G000142004

PÁDRAIG STANDÚN

LOVERS

POOLBEG

First published as *Súil le Breith* in 1983 by
Cló Chonamara, Indreabhán, Contae na Gaillimhe
This English edition, translated by the author, published by Poolbeg Press,
Knocksedan House, Swords, Co Dublin by arrangement with Cló Chonamara
Indreabhán,
Contae na Gaillimhe
Reprinted September 1991

Poolbeg Press receives financial assistance from the Arts Council/An
Chomhairle Ealaíon, Dublin. The author was the recipient of an Arts Council
bursary in 1990.

ISBN 1 85371 166 7

Cover photography by Gillian Buckley
Set by Richard Parfrey in ITC Stone Serif 10/11
Printed by Cox & Wyman Ltd Reading Berks

Paddy McEvilly was bursting for a piss, but he was too comfortable to leave the warm cocoon of blankets to relieve himself. He had six pints of Guinness the previous night and worked that trick he learned from the book the priest lent him. How many socks had been filled like that since McGahern's second novel had been published! It didn't make him guilty or ashamed any more. He had slept well until the pressure on his bladder awakened him.

It was a Sunday morning in December. The northeast wind which had blown for a week drove the Siberian cold through every crevice in the roughly-made island house, built too soon after the war. The next generation of houses were so much better.

It was a bad wind. Even though it did not bring the sea up in a swell, it made the narrow landing slip on the east side of the island very dangerous. It worried Paddy that he might have to go out to sea from there that evening. If the priest got over from the mainland village for mass, Paddy would have to help his brother-in-law to row him home again. But this might be the ill wind that would blow him good—the priest might not be able to get over at all. It was not that he had anything against Tom Connor the priest but he could do without going on the sea on such a day.

He could do without mass too though he went

regularly to please his mother. She would be in to him soon with a cup of tea and a slice of bread a scrupulous hour before mass time. She couldn't be without knowing that he had not been to confession or communion for years. Yet each Sunday morning there was this gentle (or was it insidious?) hint. It was as near as they could go to forcing religion down your throat.

In a quick movement he swung his legs out of bed and into the blue serge trousers his brother the guard had sent home to him. Shoes loose he stumbled out to the barn where he pissed loudly into the galvanised bucket his mother insisted he use as a toilet. She didn't like the smell around the backdoor, she said. More likely she didn't want old maidish Mary Guiney to see him.

"Not that she would know what it was for," he told himself out loud: she was so holy or pretended to be. He remembered the time the cow calved and she said she didn't know the difference between a bullock and a heifer. "A pity there hadn't been a man about forty years ago to show her. She couldn't have been bad-looking." A young girl wouldn't be long finding out now. But they were all gone—child-minders in Boston, civil servants in Dublin, teachers in Wexford. They had no time for the fellows that stayed at home.

Paddy was twenty-one, broad and stocky, with short curly hair and a rough-cut beard. A squint in his brown eyes gave the impression that he had a faraway look, that he was not paying attention to someone speaking directly to him. He was back on the island six years now since he was thrown out of secondary school. There were only his mother and himself left. His father was long dead, the others scattered, all except Martha, married to Patcheen John half-way back the island. They eked out a living on the widow's pension, his dole, a little fishing in the summer, a few cattle and basic crops on the eight acres of rocky limestone land.

Paddy had read a lot. It was whispered that he was a bit of a communist. It was said that he had too much influence on the young men of the island, always stirring up trouble about who would get the work on schemes promoted by the county council or the Gaeltacht Department.

"If you had a bit of spunk in you," he was told one night in the bar, "you'd be beyant in Birmingham earning big money like our lads."

"I have more to be doing with my spunk," Paddy answered, "than sweating it out through me, digging drains in England to carry away the shit of the people who can afford to have their shit piped away, while we're still doing our own under a bush."

Why did he stay, clinging like a barnacle to the grey rock? It was clear that the island was dying. While he was there it would not be let die without a kick. "Lord save us, what has got into you?" his mother said when he arrived at her bedside with a cup of steaming tea and a thick slice of buttered brown bread. She was so surprised and delighted that thickness of the bread or tarriness of the tea did not matter in the least. She looked old there in bed, her snow-white hair which he had hardly ever seen with a rib out of place, hanging loose and limp. There was a kind of musty sticky smell in the room. A lump formed in his throat and he hurried out. Why had he not thought to do something like that before?

Marion Warde snored loud and contentedly. She lay on her back, one bare arm bent across her forehead, as if she was trying to keep the sunlight out of her eyes. Her long auburn hair lay in ringlets on the pillow. She had not slept like this for years.

Propped against the pillow beside her, smoking the butt of one of the previous night's cigarettes, Tom Connor thought she was more beautiful than he had ever seen her. As she lay relaxed now, the intensity that gave her face a somewhat strained look was gone. The dark eyelashes hid the flashing black eyes. In their couple of years together he had not seen her sleep as contentedly as this.

For once the previous night his erection had survived her threshing thrusting pelvis long enough to make her come in a crying clawing climax that drained the strength from her every nerve and pore. They lay, legs threaded together, shattered by the simultaneous exploding climax. Marion gave him one big kiss and fell, literally fell, asleep. No booze, no sleeping pills. Deep sleep.

Any other morning he would be tempted to stay in bed until the last possible moment. On Sunday mornings, however, he was always on edge, nervous because of the sermon he would have to deliver, once in Irish, once in English. He had once heard a priest claim that having to give a sermon was as good as a laxative. He believed it. What was it he had prepared to say the night before? It had sounded good then, but would it be insipid in the cold light of the morning? The different languages were an added difficulty, English being spoken on the mainland part of his parish, Gaelic or Irish on the island.

His Irish was poor when he came first, but he liked the language and was trying to learn it as well as possible. Even yet the big temptation was to translate directly rather than discipline himself to think in Irish. He knew at the same time that his listeners would understand English better than bad Irish but if he spoke English on the island the Irish lobby in Dublin and Maynooth would have him castrated or worse. They weren't much help though in preparing someone for such a ministry or in supporting his efforts to better the lot of the people. He acknowledged that some of the blame was his own for not being better prepared in the language. As a student he didn't have time to go to the Gaeltacht. He had spent the holiday periods working in England to help pay his way through college.

He went down to the kitchen and lit the gas, put on the kettle. Face and teeth washed, he peered out through the lifting darkness of the winter morning. Would they be able to bring him across? The sea did not look too bad. The twin hills of the island on the horizon always reminded him of a woman's breasts, one young and full, the other shrivelled and slack. They were two great hills of limestone joined by the shallow valley in which the fifty or so houses and the little fertile land in the place were situated. The locals called it "The Island" at all times, even though it was listed in the geography books as "The Stacks."

"The Village" was in its own way an island, a green oasis in the great wasteland of nearly barren limestone stretching for twenty miles or more on every side. The villagers had at least the lifeline of thirty miles of winding road to the city, while the islanders had to come in in their currachs for shopping in the village.

Although they lived by the sea it could not be said that either community lived off it. Neither had a sheltered harbour. No boat could be used other than the currach, which could be carried inshore. Lobster was caught in the summer, down by the cliff-face to the south of the village, mackerel when the shoals came in. Since the mid-thirties there had been no large-scale fishing done, not summer and winter as in the old days before de Valera gave the dole.

The main link between the two communities was the priest. In all but the worst of weather he was rowed from one place to the other for mass every Sunday, each family taking it in turn to bring him across. It amused Tom to think that it was not because of any particular skill or capability a priest was picked for that position. It usually fell to whoever was newly ordained or available at the time, or—it is said—whoever needed a while in a punishment station to cool his heels.

Marion stirred and groaned when he brought her in tea. "What time is it?"

"Half eight. You can lie on this morning—I won't be here to keep an eye on you."

"Sit beside me, love."

"I'm in a hurry. The shepherd has to feed his sheep."

"Yourself and your sheep. A bloody ram all right."

"I have to be off."

"Just one minute. Sure I won't see you for two days."

"I have to stay there tonight—to give fair play to the island women as well."

"If you as much as look at any of them!"

"You can look at the menu, even if you're on a diet."

"Some diet you're on! I could sleep for a week." She yawned.

"Sleep on now and take your rest."

"Isn't it you that's becoming the poet all of a sudden."

"That's scripture for you. It's what Jesus said to the apostles in the garden of Gethsemane. It's what justifies the likes of me taking life easy."

"If your life is easy, I'd like to see what's hard."

"Would you now?"

"You dirty thing." Marion pulled the clothes over her head. Tom pulled them off the bed and tickled her. "Fuck off," she screeched. "One last kiss," he said.

"Don't say that. You'll frighten me."

"Sorry."

"Say one for me."

"OK." He blew her a kiss, and set out for the chapel.

Marion had for years been striding through his dreams, a tall girl with a shock of loose hair, in a long blue corduroy jacket and green trousers. It was in the sixties that they had worked together in a centre in London's Kentish Town which helped people addicted to alcohol and drugs. He was a student for the priesthood at the time, doing voluntary work at weekends, the week spent working for the Green Murphy, out from Camden Town tube station. Marion was recovering from heroin addiction at the time. He had found it hard to understand how a young girl from the west of Ireland could find herself in such a situation.

Although they were both from much the same part of Mayo, their backgrounds were quite different. Marion was reared in a council estate in town. Her father had a drink problem, her mother suffered from "nerves."

Tom was reared by an aunt and uncle in the country, neither of them married. They had taken him when his father and mother had both died young. Money was scarce, but they had their own potatoes and vegetables and killed the odd hen or pig for meat. He had never known a day's hunger and, apart from the years he spent in boarding-school, he couldn't remember anything from his youth except happiness.

They were both shy when they first met in London, but with the intuition peculiar to the shy they seemed to understand each other. Tom idolised Marion with the intense infatuation of the celibate. Her drained face reminded him of some eastern icon. He liked the way she dressed and the way she rolled cigarettes like a man.

They found themselves thrown together more and more. Together they fetched leftover bread from the bakery and carried it back to the centre, he, with awkward gallantry, insisting on carrying her share. Together they would scrounge from the Queen's Crescent market in the evenings. They crawled under stalls to retrieve burst tomatoes and lost potatoes. They waved and winked at each other beneath the tables. They rejoiced together in the acquisition of a box of over-ripe bananas from a sympathetic stall-holder. Together they went to the big Swiss Cottage swimming complex, where he floundered in the wake of her long white body, as she swam deftly between the swimmers in the crowded pool.

Once in a pub she talked of her mainlining days. All her friends from that time seemed to be dead. That evening he caught her hand when the lights changed as they were about to cross a street. She held on to his hand all the way home. It became a habit when they were out together.

When he got up one morning Marion was gone, and it was ten years before he saw her again. The others in the centre taunted him, asked how did he manage without it. He wondered was she back on the drugs or gone to some man. He was fairly sure she left so as not to interfere with his priestly vocation.

Maybe she was taken from his path to let him continue on the straight and narrow path of celibacy. He had little faith in that kind of *deus ex machina*, but supposed it was not beyond the bounds of possibility. But that kind of logic would suggest it was God that brought them together again. Did that make the Lord into some kind of puppeteer, and leave a person without freedom?

For the rest of his working holiday he had walked London's streets, sometimes taking the 24 bus through town, looking out for that familiar loping walk, the long curling hair and the corduroys. Her image had haunted him for many years in the long corridors of Maynooth.

Bridgie Hughie lived in the farthest cottage west in the island, nearly halfway up the Cruach Theas, where there was a beautiful view of the western sea, the green Atlantic whitening itself on the barely-submerged rock. Bridgie was eighty-four. She had never married. She could not read or write, speak or understand English. She had no radio and had never seen a television set. For as long as anyone remembered she had been considered *aisteach* —a bit strange. Many's the person would have liked to help her, but she made it clear that she had no welcome for anyone but the priest with holy communion on the first Friday of the month.

She moved out from time to time. She would sweep into a house, her long petticoats brushing the floor. She would sit on a hob or a stool by a range, gathering her red skirts around her, and, hugging her knees close to her chest, talk for hours as if weeks of silence were escaping from a bottle.

Children were wary of her. They treated her as they would treat an untrustworthy dog that would be all over you today and bite the hand off you tomorrow. The fault was not all on her side.

Young boys delighted in taunting her from a safe distance, wolf-whistling from behind walls as she made her slow way to the shop. They had good reason to keep their distance from her blackthorn stick. She had nearly maimed one of the Reillys once with it. He tripped as he ran away after calling her names.

At nine o'clock that Sunday morning Bridgie was doubled up with a terrible pain in her chest. She was very cold and there was a queer kind of pain in her head as well. All the clothes in the house were piled on top of her. She was too paralysed with pain and cold to try lighting the fire. Despite the cold, sweat stood in droplets on her forehead. Her spindly arms worked in circular movements, her fists opening and closing, gripping the blankets in an effort to ease the pain. A querulous piping sound came from her lips, like the noise made by a cornered hare as dogs move in for the kill. There was nobody listening.

She knew that there had been something wrong with the taste of the salted mackerel she had eaten the evening before. It must have been that that did the damage. She had not eaten anything else for two days. What could she have eaten? The last cake had been gnawed down to the crust by the rats. She was not able to go to the shop. You didn't see much of the neighbours when you needed them, though they were under your feet until you signed over the land. She gathered her strength to put the curse of God on Patcheen John, the nearest relative she had, the man she signed the land to. By the time she got round to cursing him she had forgotten what she wanted to do.

She was a young girl again, in the currach with her father. She had held a squirming mackerel to die in her hands. She felt the salt mackerel in her stomach was exacting some sort of revenge. Images from her youth swam before her eyes, a supple girl with red skirts tied up to her waist as she carried baskets of seaweed from the tide for the kelp-making. Michael was there too, a tall boy about her own age. It was he who helped her mother when her father was drowned on the way home from the kelp market in the village. "Poteen," people had whispered. Bridgie never went to school after that.

Those were the best times. When they were seventeen and eighteen she and Michael used to walk together on the Cruach Mhór and sit on the heather in the summer sunshine. One day the red priest stopped them as they came down the hill and told them they would be married on Shrove Tuesday. He did not want any scandals in his parish. There had been enough of them before his time.

Michael rowed over to the village on his own that night. He made his way to Boston. There he had died a couple of years ago. They said his grandson was a priest. Bridgie had been on her own in that little thatched house since her mother died, half a century or more before. She had not wanted anyone when her first love was gone. Life was hard but she survived. She was not bothered by gales or high seas, by sickness or by worry. She never left the island.

Dogs and cats she had in plenty. They grew up and grew old. They died. "Pity there isn't one of them now to slaughter the rats." She had the soreness again, worse than before. A thin piping squeal came from her lips. She remembered there was a drop of poteen in the press. It might kill the pain.

The village mass was over about half past nine. Tom Connor was taking off his vestments when there was a quick nervous knocking on the sacristy door. It was the "*fear a' turn*," the next man on the rota to bring the priest across to the island. Tom had heard the same term used in Inis Oírr and Inis Meáin in the Aran islands of Galway Bay. All the old men had stories of days they were on the "turn" themselves, still remembering in vivid detail the state of the wind and the tide, the wetness or the contrariness of the priest.

"Not a great morning, Father." A quick swipe of his hand snapped the cap respectfully from his head.

"Not great at all, John. What is the sea like?"

"Sure there's no sea at all in it. The wind isn't the best."

"Well, if we can't go we can't go."

"I'm not saying we can't go."

"You'll have a go at bringing me across so."

"A bit of a north-east wind never did anyone any harm."

"I'll be down so inside the half-hour."

"Bring plenty of clothes, Father. It'll be cold on the sea today. What about the bag? Will I go up for the bag?"

"I'll carry that down myself. There's no weight in it."

The bag in question was a battered old duffle-bag he used to carry his clothes in the currach, as well as altar breads and wine when he needed them. He knew that it was from genuine respect for the office of priest people offered to carry his bag or his coat. Still he felt it was making a lady or something of a squireen out of him, the kind of forelock-touching obeisance the landlords got in the old days. Had the Roman Catholic clergy made the same kind of pseudo-aristocrats of themselves? There were some who felt so and also felt they would have the same sort of natural death.

Tom took with him his oilskin coat and trousers as well as the bag and set out to walk the half-mile to the seashore. The men had already carried down the currach, and were now checking the oars and *cnogaí*, the oaken tholepins the oars revolved on. Although they often used an outboard motor on the transom of the currach many of the men preferred to row, especially in a wind. The engine suited the priest better because it meant that he had his back to the wind. The spray of the waves would hit his back, rather than chest, as happened when he was seated in the stern of the currach with three men rowing. As he neared the shore Tom noticed that the currach was rigged up to carry a sail, something that was done occasionally when they would have the wind behind them. It would help sweep the currach along as quickly as any sail-boat.

"Is there any bit of a woman back there on the island that would suit Big Mick here?" Pádraic Mhichilín asked the priest. Mick Macken was a big strong porter-headed man in his fifties, a powerful seaman who lived alone at the east end of the village. "If he talks nice to you, you might give him one of your own daughters." He knew that the chances of one of the frail-looking sexy Michilíns coming back from Manchester to marry big toothless Mick were very slight. "Maybe myself and yourself are better off without the women, Father." Mick gave a burst of embarrassed laughing, and Tom Connor felt that he was blushing himself.

All four of them got a grip on the currach and dragged it down the sand to the water's edge. A bag of sand was put in for ballast. Mick crossed over the seats, sat on the one nearest the prow and readied the oars. He was considered one of the greatest oarsmen in living memory. John, the *"fear a' turn"*, was put in the middle. Apart from his yearly trip on the turn he didn't have much rowing practice. He didn't feel at home talking to a priest, a job he left to Pádraic Mhichilín, who could talk to the Pope if he had to.

When the currach was almost afloat, the priest got into the third seat and Pádraic pushed off. Then they exchanged places. Pádraic blessed himself, put out his oars and all three of them began to row steadily. Pádraic was a big man, almost sixty now, still very strong. He and his wife, Cáit, had raised a big family, all of whom were away working, apart from Barbara, who was in boarding-school in the city, and Teresa, who was seventeen and mentally handicapped. She lived with them at home.

When they rowed out of the shelter of the land and

into the wind, a triangular black sail was hoisted. Pádraic went into the stern again and used the oar as a rudder. They clipped along over the choppy waves as fast as any outboard engine would drive them, the two men in front barely touching the water with quick oar strokes.

Very few of the local seamen could swim. None of them ever wore a life-jacket. There was a saying that the currach carrying the priest would not sink. It had not happened so far although they had been close enough to it on a few occasions over the years. Tom Connor was not sure was it faith or superstition but he didn't want to be the one to prove the old saying wrong. He could swim reasonably well but in a broken sea the ability to swim might just prolong the agony. The nearest lifeboats were at least fifty miles away, in Donegal's Arranmore or Galway's Aran.

"You'll have a tough time coming back against it, Pádraic."

"It won't be so bad. There is no swell in it and the wind will probably drop by and by. We were thinking of staying on for a while, to taste the island porter. There's a nice salty taste on it after crossing the sea. None of us was here for a long time, and we might fix Mick up with a woman."

"Do you ever be afraid on the sea, Father?"

"No, not as long as I don't see the men on the turn getting nervous themselves."

"Isn't that wonderful too—someone raised so far from the sea…"

"I used be afraid all right at the beginning. When I'd see a big wave coming I'd say to myself that this must be the last one. The 'O my God' was often on my lips.

But we would go over it or through it, and I'd begin to breathe again. Until the next one."

"It's for those kind of seas the currach was made."

"I know that now, but it took a good while."

"Some of the priests long ago were awful hard men, Father."

"What's so soft about the ones that are around now?"

"Ah, you know well what I'm saying. Things are changed, thanks be to God. Nowadays you leave it to the man whose turn it is to decide if it's fit to cross. In the old days it's many the priest made men put out a currach against their better judgement."

It seemed as if the sea was getting choppier. Pádraic explained the direction of the tides. Then he started to reminisce.

"I remember the first turn I was ever on, thirty-five, nearer to forty, years ago. They're all dead now, the men that were with me, the priest too..."

It looked as if the currach was going to capsize: the wind seemed to lean on the sail as they were facing into a couple of towering waves with a deep trough between them. Pádraic deftly manoeuvred the prow to take them, speaking all the while through teeth clenched on the mouthpiece of his pipe.

"It was a terrible day. There was a south-east wind blowing waves crosswise on that little slip we'll be going in on in a few minutes. We were waiting outside the breaking wave, waiting for time, for an easy break. You know what it's like yourself. The people of the island stood way back, waving at us to go home. They know that landing place better than we do. Father Daly, *An Dálach Mór*, that was with us. A nice man, he knew nothing about the sea. I'm not wronging the man now that he's dead. He was a brave man, but it's a different thing being brave with someone else's life. I wasn't married at the time, but the other two had wives and children. 'We'll go in, in the name of God,' Father Daly said. That was the time you would do what a priest said, right or wrong. We chanced it when there was half a break. Next thing we noticed was the islanders running away from the slip. The biggest breaker of a wave you ever saw was rising like a cliff outside us. 'This is the end,' I said to myself, but there was no time to be thinking of it. We tried to race it in, get in before it, but what good was that? It swept the currach with it like a matchbox and landed it in at the top of the slip, upside down on top of us. The people of the island dragged us in by arms and legs as the backwash swept out the currach. The next wave made matches of it on the rocks. When we had time to look around us there was Father Daly searching in his pocket. We thought he had lost something. We were standing there looking at him. 'I thought I might at least have caught a fish,' he said. He was a funny man. It was a week before the weather settled enough for us to go home."

They were nearing the island now and the sail was lowered. As usual there were men and boys waiting, shouting instructions above the waves in high-pitched voices. "There's two more in it," Mick said. Tom could see nothing different on the surface of the sea but sure enough two large waves soon passed beneath them. "Now, now..." the islanders shouted. The currach was swung around and rowed in backwards to the spot where four men had waded into the sea to snatch it away from the next wave.

The travellers got out of the currach. The priest took off his oilskins and wellingtons, put on his walking shoes. His crew talked and joked with the men of the island as they pulled the boat in from any possible danger from the tide. Talk was of the weather, the price of cattle and the coming Christmas. "Would there be many coming home?"

The next in line for the turn on the island, Patcheen John, was down to carry up the priest's bag. They then set out quickly for the chapel, Tom trying to warm himself after sitting for almost an hour, cold in the currach.

"Nothing new, Patcheen, I suppose?"

"Devil the thing, Father. Things be very quiet at this time of the year."

"Ah well, Christmas is on the way."

"With the help of God."

The young men beneath the gallery were having great crack. While there was no girl between the age of twelve and thirty on the island at that time of the year, there were up to twenty men in that age-group. Some would be coming in for the bit of land at home, others waiting until they were old enough to set out for Birmingham or Boston. Most had done a few years at secondary school taking advantage of the free education that had started in the sixties. They showed little interest in academic subjects, and found life in a city boarding-school alien. Most left before their Inter-Cert examinations.

Theirs was a harmless sort of crack that relieved the boredom of standing quietly through mass. There was some pushing and pinching, imitation of the priest's accent and the way he pronounced some words in the Munster dialect. It was not that they didn't believe, just that they felt bored and awkward. Jackie Reilly got on his knees and rocked back and forth in the manner of some of the older men. One of the Fitzgeralds, home for his father's funeral of a couple of weeks earlier, pinched Paddy McEvilly's ear. The response was a loudly-whispered "Fuck off." Heads turned. There were sighs of disapproval from the seats in front of them.

It was not that Paddy was interested in what the priest was doing up at the altar. He was thinking of Janet Woods, a journalist who had spent a couple of weeks on the island the previous year. Someone, probably the priest, had sent her to Paddy to discover the views of the younger people about the future of the island. She was not young and you couldn't say she was beautiful, but there was something about her that attracted him. She was a big woman who wore jumpers and jeans that seemed too tight for her. At least Paddy thought so.

She knew how to write, though, not like some of the writers and journalists who spent a couple of days on the island from time to time, and then wrote expert articles about peace, contentment, and, of course, the clichéd, "*ciúnas gan uaigneas,*" quietness without loneliness. They wrote of the beautiful people who lived in a paradise without cars, without electricity, without television, doctor, priest or policeman. "Some paradise," thought Paddy on reading one such article. "No women."

Janet had got a good picture of the humanity and the reality of the place, the problems of bachelorhood, boredom, drink, depression, the petty hatreds and long memories, the desire for revenge so strong in any small country place. She balanced the picture with stories of the advantages of the free and easy life.

Her article had not gone down well locally. "No one ever wrote anything bad about us before," people said. "No one ever wrote the truth before," Paddy had said in a pub argument about the article. Of course he got the blame for it all—it was he who had been drinking with her every night.

It was not what she had written he was thinking of now but of the last night she had spent on the island. He had had a feed of porter, she of vodka. Neither was steady on the feet. They enjoyed taking the two sides of the road with them as he left her back to her digs, pretending they were more drunk than they were. They stood, a hundred yards or so from where she was staying, their arms about each other. "It's a pity you can't come with me," she said. "You could teach a lot to the whizz-kids up in the office."

"I'd be like a fish out of water."

"I think you'd make your way anywhere. I'm afraid you're wasting away your life here. From listening to you for the last fortnight I know what you think of the island. But what real chance have you of changing anything? It's like trying to turn the tide back with a fork. You don't stand a chance."

"I got the impression during the week that you weren't too satisfied with life in the city yourself."

"True enough, but I couldn't live without people around me, without pubs, without theatres, without shows."

"That's the difference between us. I don't belong to the city middle class."

"Forget about class. It doesn't exist any more. Everyone is the same now."

"The same? The rich and the poor, the salaried and the subsidised? Charity!"

"Yourself and your charity. I'll give you charity if you're not careful." She snuggled closer to him, only to be held away at arm's length.

"That's exactly what it would be—if you were to give it to me, charity to the barbarian, the noble savage. I've read the sociology books too."

"I don't see you as a barbarian, and I don't give charity to anyone, not the kind of charity you are thinking of anyway."

"Am I expected to cry?"

"Cry your nuff. You won't find much of that here, and I'm not talking of myself. What chance have you of ever getting a wife here, even if you live to be a hundred?"

"It would be a bit late then anyway, though it might not, when I wouldn't have used it until that."

"It's impossible to talk to you tonight."

"You're full of pity for me. But for all your talk did you get a man, big and all as the city is?" She couldn't see his smile.

"That's not very fair. But if you want to know I got enough of them. Too many."

"But none of them were as nice as me." He put his hand up under her jumper, inside her bra. They kissed. Janet firmly took Paddy's hand away, touched his cheek, said "Goodnight. This place won't be finished as long as you are here."

She was gone then in the darkness. Paddy waited until he saw the door close behind her. There were few nights since that he had not thought of those big breasts under that tight blue sweater. What she had said to him reverberated in his consciousness even more. Maybe he was wasting his time staying on the island.

The consecration bell awoke Paddy from his daydream. Looking around him it was obvious that not everyone's mind was wandering. The vast majority of people were following everything the priest said or did at the altar. For them it was the most important half-hour in the week, the Last Supper and Calvary rolled into one, Christ's victory over sin and death, a commemoration of the opening of heaven's gates to humanity, letting people live forever with God, if that is what they choose.

Tom Connor, at the altar, contemplated the chalice and paten before him and what they contained. What a leap of faith it took to see there the presence of Christ in the Eucharist. What wonder, what beautiful simplicity. That is what he firmly believed, what most of his congregation believed. "Do this in memory of me," Jesus had said in the Upper Room. That's what they were doing.

"God, I'm here almost a year." Marion was talking out loud to herself as she often did when there was no one around. She had had a lovely lazy day, lying in bed, reading a while, smoking a few cigarettes. She couldn't be bothered with food on a day like that. She left the bed long enough to watch the currach make its way west to the island. Tom was part of that black spot bouncing on the ocean. She felt that if anything happened to him it would be the end of her. It was not that she had not got over worse. Things got harder to put up with every time. Adversity doesn't harden. It just brings the possibility of cracking up nearer.

Rats or mice or bats or birds pattered about in the room immediately over her head. Let them be. Poison didn't seem to bother them. If anything they seemed to thrive on it. Some day they might eat each other up. Maybe that was the philosophy behind that particular poison, psychological warfare. Generation for annihilation. Extermination by procreation. She would have to tell Tom that one.

The size of the house seemed to fit it for something other than a celibate priesthood. If anything it suggested a harem. There were thirteen rooms. It was an old coastguard station. The parish had bought it for £100 in 1921. That had probably saved it from being burned. There were big cold rooms, bars still on some windows. It reminded Marion of a prison when she was depressed.

They used only three rooms—two really since she had started to sleep with Tom. The third had a made-up bed for appearances' sake. Having to keep up appearances made her sick. Hypocrisy. Pretence. Respectable veneer. Still, mostly she was happy here. Call it a common-law marriage of convenience. Call it love. Call it sin, living over the sticks. Call it anything you like. It had worked so far.

Strange that they had met again. Her youngest sister had married Tom's cousin. Marion had come back for the wedding, her first time home in eleven years. Caroline, her little sister, was only nine years old when she herself had left home. She had always loved Caroline, looked on her as the bright side of her home.

Caroline, named after a princess a couple of generations out of a Mayo bog. Delusions of grandeur. She
was the pride of the family, the only one to finish her
education, a schoolteacher. She had sent her money
from England as often as she could, even when she had
very little herself. It helped. One of them had made it,
in spite of the home and the continuous fights between
mother and father.

Even that had improved, things were so much better now than when she was a child. She had hated the
boozing, the nagging, the insults, the beatings. Maybe
it was the big family: perhaps they couldn't take the
pressure. She knew more about life now. They often
went out together now to lounge-bars, whispered like
young ones in love. The fact that her father had to ease
off on the drink because of his health helped. It had
quietened and mellowed him.

Tom had celebrated the wedding mass. She knew
him from somewhere. It took a while to come back.
Kentish Town, Simon. So long ago. He had aged well.

He had recognised her straight away, shy until he
had a few jars in him. They had talked, danced. She
had not danced for ages. She hadn't wanted to go back
to London. She needed time to pull herself together, to
get over some bad experiences with men. She was so
fed up with men she had thought she could live like a
nun. "Why don't you come back with me, look after
me for a while?" he had said. Why not!

When she saw the house she thought she would
not stay a week. The local people made her welcome,
seemed to be pleased Tom had help and companion-
ship. Maybe they saw her as a prospect for a bachelor
son.

For a while they had lived a blissful platonic love. Never fought once. She had put shape on the place, cleaned—how it had needed it—painted using bright pastel shades, replaced the dowdy curtains, made the place liveable. Tom protested, too much of a socialist for his own comfort, hers either. But he was pleased at the end result.

They prepared the meals together. She taught him all she knew about cooking, Chinese, Indian, French. He claimed the garlic was putting people off confession, destroying his business, as he put it. They laughed and talked a lot. It was like a rest from real life, like living on the edge of the world and not looking in: Tír na nÓg, a dream. The lovemaking was inevitable.

Little Margaret Jack Phaddy showed her book to the priest. She was two and a half, and he often told her she was his favourite girl on the island.

"We'll have a rest now that the babysitter is back," Margaret's mother, Mary, said. She was in her early thirties, a little overweight. "Pregnant again," Tom thought, "At least there's a bigger break between Margaret and the new one than between the others." He liked Jack and Mary. It was in their house he stayed the nights he spent on the island. Jack was fond of his pint but kind and hard-working.

There were so many of themselves in the house that Tom didn't know how they were able to make a room available for him. But it was there the priests had always stayed, and you couldn't offer Jack Phaddy a bigger insult than to change to another lodgings. He was building an extension to the house, and Tom helped him by mixing concrete when he was there o weekends.

"Will you be down, Tom?" Jack asked, "down" meaning the only pub on the island. "No, Jack. Not now. Tonight maybe."

"Ah, come on. This is the best time for the crack, after mass on Sunday."

"Sure I'd only be in the way and ye finding fault with the sermon I gave this morning."

"You don't think anyone listens!"

"Don't you know well Jack listens to no one but himself," Mary said.

"The women always have the last word."

"Why don't you go on so—if I've said the last word."

"I'm worrying about the two of you—why are you trying to get rid of me." Mary started to blush.

"That fellow would say anything."

"Come on down, Tom. Can't you come again to-night?"

"I have to see a couple of people this evening. Anyway I've rosary and benediction. It wouldn't do to be drunk at that."

"Damn all harm it would do. It would give some of them ould wans something to talk about. They're lost without a bit of a scandal. It's years since there was a girl up the pole or anything. Of course when there isn't any girl..."

"Such talk before the priest. Thanks be to God the rest of the children are out playing."

"Isn't it a pity Geraldine isn't here. She's the one for the questions. 'What's 'up the pole', Mammy?' No bother to Mammy to explain, and she up the pole again herself."

"Get going," she said in mock anger. "He's awful, Father. What will he say next?"

"She's up the pole alright, Connor, and you thinking I had no spunk left in me. There's life in the old dog yet."

"The shakings of the bag," Mary said.

"More than the bag."

"Get out." She reached for the tongs.

"One day she's trying to keep me home from the pub. The next day she's driving me out with the tongs. You're a witness to this, Connor."

Jack went off laughing. Mary began to prepare the dinner. "Walkies." Margaret took Tom's finger and led him towards the door. They wandered back the road together, a tall thin man and a small rotund girl waddling beside him.

"You've the right job now, Father." said Marcas Phaddy, after he had heaped the blessings of God on them. A small man, face weather-beaten and wrinkled, eyes sparkling behind round glasses.

"Isn't the weather very cold, Father."

"Too cold, I think, for this little woman to be out walking, Marcas."

"Into the house with you, so. I've a letter to show you."

Margaret was not very pleased that her walk ended so quickly. Mary put the two men into the sitting-room and switched on the gas heater for them. Tom went looking for a half-bottle of whiskey he had put aside for just such an occasion but it was not to be found. Jack must have needed a cure, he thought.

"Well, Father, I wouldn't be bothering you at all, except for this *diabhal* of a letter I got from the Land

Commission the other day. Could they be serious about it? What have we but the biteen of land?"

The letter was stark and to the point. It was a bill for two pounds and eleven pence rent. Unless it was paid immediately, Marcas's land would be put on the open market.

The people of the island had no rates to pay, but there was a small rental annuity due to the Land Commission since the Land Acts at the beginning of the century. Marcas hadn't paid for a number of years because the commission would not change the title of the land from his grandfather's name. He could not afford a solicitor so he hoped to force the hand of the commission by refusing the miserly rent.

The letter angered the priest, anger that showed in his voice. "I'm a long time dealing with civil servants, and a lot of them are less than civil, but I haven't come across the likes of this yet. I know they are entitled to look for money, but threatening to put someone out of house and home for the price of a plug of tobacco... The landlords were bad enough!"

"Don't let Maggie hear you talk of landlords. Her father and mother were thrown out on the side of the road a couple of months before she was born."

"Don't worry, Marcas. You won't be thrown out while I'm alive."

"Would you put the money in the post for me from the village, Father, when you get home. I'd like to go home and be able to say to Maggie you're looking after it and everything will be all right. Her heart is not the best, you know."

"I'd prefer to help you fight your case, but it's your land, and I don't want to give them any chance of it."

"Whatever you think yourself, Father. We'll follow your advice. We always followed the advice of the priests."

"Do you know what I'll do, and it'll suit both of us. I'll pay the bill. But I'll write a strong letter to the paper opposing this sort of threatening letter. I'll say it would suit them better to be putting the titles of the land in order."

"I'd prefer if you didn't mention my name in the paper. Maggie, y'know. It might frighten her."

"I had no notion of mentioning your name, Marcas."

"We don't want any kind of trouble. One of the lads—I don't think you ever met Jim. He's talking of coming home in a couple of years. We'd like him to have the land, so he could look after us in the latter years. He might even marry."

"Don't worry, Marcas. No one will take away your land. I'll put the money in the post tomorrow evening."

"Pay it out of that, and have the rest for a drink." He left ten pounds on the table.

"That's far too much, Marcas. I was going to look after that myself."

"Do what I tell you now. You've been very good to us. *Go bhfága Dia againn thú.* May God leave you with us. Sure Maggie is always talking about you."

When Marcas was gone, Tom decided to get down to writing the letter while the mood of indignation was still on him. In the strongest language he could muster he complained not just about the commission's letter, but the attitude behind it—a lack of sensitivity to the old and to the weakest people in society. While he was at it he had a lash at the trade unions, whom he admired for their commitment to their members but who should in his opinion be doing much more for the unemployed and people on such supplementary benefit as the small farmers' dole.

He had applied for dole himself the previous year. He felt he would be entitled to it if he took nothing from the parish monies for himself. In that way he hoped to draw attention to the fact that in his parish, only the shopkeeper, the nurse, the teacher and the priest did not depend on the dole. He felt the state owed him a salary of some kind, as they used him to keep the law, to manage the school, to fill pension and dole forms. Was he ordained to be a buckshee civil servant?

For four months he had received through the post the square brown social welfare envelope with the economy sticker, the stigma of the deprived, the subsidised, the new poor.

At last the gauger came to assess his means. The gauger is the name given in the west to the social welfare inspector. A nice man, he questioned Tom about his income from mass stipends and collections, and where and how money was spent. With a little smile playing around his mouth, he told Tom he might be entitled to fifty pence a week. A few days later he had a letter from Bishop Caufield, however he had got to know of it, telling him to withdraw his application. There must have been a Knight of Columbanus or two tied up in red tape, he thought. Although he did not withdraw, he didn't hear any more from the Social Welfare Department.

After his meal Tom took a long walk on the *creig* on the south-west of the island, where there was shelter from the wind. Watching the waves breaking on the shoreline contented him always. He had never dreamt in college that a priest could be as happy in his work as he was. He often wondered about the cross, how there had never been a heavy one laid on his shoulders. His parents' deaths? He had never known them. His uncle and aunt had been as good as parents could be.

Little had he thought on his first day in the parish that he would settle in so well. He remembered the day the bishop had summoned him to his office. In a newspaper article Tom had criticised the type of secondary boarding-school he worked in. He saw no justification for having ten and more priests teach in such colleges, "so-called minor seminaries" he called them. If there was a real shortage of priests and an unemployment crisis in the teaching profession, why were priests keeping lay people out of work? Was it their vocation to baby-sit the children of the rich?

The bishop sat behind a scrupulously-neat oak table. He was a small fat man, bald, bespectacled, his hands joined on the table before him. His reputation was not that of being an old-fashioned hard bishop, but one of the new breed, consecrated, as one wag put it, not just by the Church, but by the media as well. He had made his name in parish work as a great churchbuilder, a man who took the long-term view, and insisted on good-quality artwork and stained windows, whatever the cost. Nothing was too good for the house of God. A good GAA man, he had, despite his size, been the terror of many an inter-county defence in his youth. Only clerical law of the time had deprived him of an All-Ireland medal. As a young priest in the fifties his reputation for scattering courting couples

was legendary. In recent times he rejoiced in the reputation of being "a great man for the women," laughing
loudly at after-confirmation dinners when through the
cigar smoke his canons joked about this.

"You have let me down again, Tom."

"Let you down, David?" It was first-name stuff.
"Boot in the balls, knife in the back stuff," Tom thought.

"You know what I'm talking about. No need to beat
about the bush. That article was uncalled for."

"Was it theologically inaccurate, or what?"

"Damn well you know it's not anything like that.
You're too cute a hoor to make that sort of mistake. I
know you are sound enough on the theological score—
at least, I think you are."

"I appreciate your confidence in me, David."

"Sarcasm doesn't become you, Tom. That's exactly
what I'm talking about. Your whole attitude to me, to
authority. Even before you were ordained, in Maynooth,
you showed scant respect for authority. Did you know that
I ordained you against the advice of the college authorities?"

"I'm grateful."

"Don't mention it. If you were to see the letters I
have got since that article came out. Letters from canons, from parish priests, from curates not much older
than yourself, from lay past pupils, professional men,
the cream of society." He struck the table with a pudgy
fist. "They are up in arms because you insulted their
college, our college. They're looking for your…"

"And they'll get them."

"There it is again. You are not able to listen. I have
to live with these men, men who have given their
whole lives to the Church. Why are you never able to
accept the views of the *maior et senior pars*. Why have

you to be always out of line—everyone out of step except our Tom."

"I try to say what I believe."

"Isn't that what we're all trying to do; but there are ways and means…"

"There are, but who listens?"

"They listened to you alright. They love your anti-clerical bullshit." He stopped. He lit himself a cigarette, without offering one to Tom. He then looked him between the eyes. "I have a job for you, Tom. Kilcronan. Mainland and island. Administrator, your own boss, after me, of course. Father Máirtín is long enough out there. *He* would enjoy a while in the college now…" He giggled "Baby-sitting." Serious again, "You'll be very happy out there, when you get used to the Irish. Take it easy on the pen for a while, until you understand the ways of the Church a bit better. If you intend to stay in this diocese. By the way, why don't you write in Irish? Write whatever you like in Irish, so few read it anyway…" He reached out his hand. "May God go with you, Tom."

"Judas," said Tom under his breath, as he shook hands. He walked out. "Kilcronan, the arsehole of the diocese, and you'll be the shit in that hole," was the verdict of one of his fellow-priests in the college, a verdict delivered with some relish.

Although he arrived in the middle of winter the place and the people appealed to him from the beginning. The islanders did not shame him for his broken Irish, just put the correct words and phrases into his mouth. Although scared of the sea from time to time he revelled in the challenge the crossing posed. He liked too the notoriety his banishment gave him among fellow-priests and parishioners. It gave him a freedom—he couldn't be banished any further.

His one regret was the fact that he was living a lie as far as his private life was concerned, a married man at home, a celibate priest in the eyes of his parishioners. It was not that he saw any sense in compulsory celibacy. He had never taken the vow of celibacy very seriously. He wanted to serve God as a priest. The fact that in the present dispensation priests were not allowed marry was an unfortunate part of a package deal he had reluctantly accepted.

He had long come to the conclusion that the only way to change the law of celibacy was contrary custom, a principle enshrined in canon law. If enough priests lived with women, the Church could not sack them all. They would have to take account of the reality. According to surveys the majority of the world's priests believed there should be an option to marry, but because of the present law the only way men could marry was to leave the priesthood. Did not the practice of the other Churches prove that a man could be a good priest as well as a husband and father?

Living with Marion did not afflict Tom's conscience. Deluding his congregation did, pulling the wool over the eyes of those people who were so good to him, to both of them.

Was he using Marion to fulfil his sexual needs in the guise of love? Or had the Lord sent them together to help them both? That justification was a bit too easy. Any excuse for himself. But the attack on the law of compulsory celibacy would have to come, sooner (before he got too old) rather than later.

The island pub was often passed unnoticed, because there was no sign on the outside and no indication that it was anything other than a thatched cottage. Inside it was fine and big, the whole building one big bar. The owners lived in the new bungalow opposite. The owner/barman, Johnny Collins, who married the daughter of the previous owner in England, was from County Limerick. They had plenty of pub experience, having managed a bar for Ansells in Coventry.

People thought they would never make a go of it— no one could replace old Tommy Regan. The atmosphere wouldn't be the same. It wasn't. You didn't have to wait a half-hour for your pint and the glasses were clean, nor did you have to put up with Tommy's contrariness or idiosyncratic opening and closing hours.

There had been a general amnesty for all barred customers, which really meant the Reillys who had never got on with Regan and Paddy McEvilly who didn't support the right political party and was argumentative about it. Collins had bought an electricity generator for his house and bar and installed a TV set in the corner. People said the old-timers would never put up with television but they became its biggest addicts. It also added an extra excuse for going to the pub—to watch the news. They might have a pint when they were there. Apart from tourists and some younger women home on holiday, no woman ventured into this all-male enclave. Johnny Collins had it in mind to build a lounge to try and attract some of them.

"If you were to believe the old people—" Jack Phaddy opened the evening's proceedings with a barb at Peadar Rua, an old man who came in for his weekly drink on Sunday evening, "the summers were hotter in the old days and the winters were colder. The seas used to be higher, and there were better seamen to go out on them. Do you know why that was, Father? Sure that couldn't be true." He would love, as he sat at the counter on his high stool, to get the priest and old Peadar stuck in each other.

Tom Connor, sitting with his back to the wall, would have preferred to be left in peace to drink his pint. "I don't know," he said. "Some people say that every twenty years or so you get bad winters. People talk of '47 and '63, though there was not twenty years between them. To be honest, I know nothing about it."

"Old people are like Yanks," Patcheen John said. "Everything is bigger and better where they are from, or in their time."

"I wouldn't think they were half as good as the men that are in it now." Jackie Reilly gave a young man's view.

Peadar took the bait. He gave a contemptuous spit. "Men is it?" he said, "Men with hair on them like women and a smell of perfume off them. Men with rings on their ears and bangles on their hands, red trousers on them, or purple, maybe, men that haven't much between their legs, I'd say."

"I think it's how you're jealous of long hair, Peadar—" Reilly tossed back his own lank quiff, "—seeing as your own head is as bald as a baby's arse."

"It's not jealous I am, but pitiful. I'd prefer to see hair on a man's arms or his chest, or somewhere else I'd prefer not to mention, than to see him with a head of long hair. It's not natural."

"What about the Son of God?" asked Jack Phaddy.

"They didn't have any scissors at the time, or blades

either."

"You have all the answers, Peadar."

There was no stopping the old man, however. "Show me the man today that would row a currach from morning till night with nothing in his stomach but a few cold potatoes. Where is the man that would go out in a northeast gale to bring the priest across for a sick call? We did it in my time. Ye're too soft to do it."

"And what's making people soft nowadays, Peadar?"

"Haven't they everything too easy? Sleeping all day, drinking all night. Free money from the government. Fathers and mothers spoiling them. Natural enough when they are growing up to go away, but once spoiled, spoiled for life."

"This complaining and giving out about the young people is all right for ould ones." Paddy McEvilly knew his contribution would be resented but he was angry. Sunday night was not the time for that kind of debate, but he felt he couldn't let talk like that go unchallenged. "It doesn't matter a fuck what they think of me," he said to himself.

"This kind of talk is all right, but do you think there is any young lad on this island that wants to be idle? Do you think we wouldn't work if there was work to be had? What happens when the county council has work on offer? It's the people that have enough already that get it, the people on high dole, that are as well off without work. The single fellow on his lousy little *dóilín* gets nothing.

"Listen, son," Jack Phaddy said. "It's not at a meeting of the community council you're at now." That put Paddy in his place in the eyes of the onlookers. There had been a community council set up a couple of years previously but it hadn't been much of a success. After all their talk of the lack of democracy, the government departments and the county council continued to give work to their own old friends.

The pub was quiet for a few minutes. Paddy McEvilly was livid. He would have loved to unleash the bile of his bitterness and frustration at them but wouldn't give them that satisfaction. Look at them, he wanted to say, more than half of them bachelors gone past marriage. Sitting there every Sunday for twenty, maybe forty years, letting their youth slip by, letting their seed slip through their fingers as likely as not. Did they ever think that it didn't have to be like that, that things could change, if you had the guts to change them. He was vexed too with Tom Connor, the priest, whose feelings he knew to be similar to his own. But when it came to the crunch he wasn't able to stand up to the older men.

Conversation began again in dribs and drabs.

"The wind is gone south."

"Yes. The glass has been falling the last few days."

"There'll be rain out of this, storms maybe."

"The forecast isn't good for tomorrow evening, force seven or eight."

"The gale is a dangerous latchiko."

"Wouldn't it be nice to get a fine spell around Christmas."

"With the help of God... There'll be a moon this year."

"And down the road came Sligo Kate, With her knickers in her hand." Shamey Fitz's voice broke across the low hum of Gaelic conversation. The bar was quiet for a moment; then the talk started again. "Up she flew and the cock flattened her." Shamey banged his glass on the counter, sending porter froth flying. "And she never lost a feather." There were a few smiles and giggles. No one pretended to take any notice. This kind of thing could be tolerated, while Paddy McEvilly's questioning could not.

The two Fitzs had come home from England a fortnight earlier for their father's funeral. It wasn't worth their whiles to go back until after Christmas. They had been drinking since mass time, and now stood, swaying slightly at the counter.

"Never again...never fucking again...You'll never come back, Pat." Shamey looked around the bar, full to the door with men, most of them in grey homespun clothes, so different from their own light well-made brightly-coloured suits.

For two homesick years Shamey had looked forward to coming home, rowing west as the sun was sinking. The place was changed. It was not just the funeral that had upset him. The bastards had hardly noticed he had been away, that he was back from England, a man. He was a stranger here now, but without the respect shown to strangers. He understood better than ever now that old catchphrase of the Irish in England: "You'll never go back now, Pat."

He looked around at the "lads", the same "lads" that were in it when he was a boy. They were wearing their years well, the fucking wankers, the lazy good-for-nothing wastrels, paid to live out here by a hypocritical government, all in the cause of "culture" and the Irish language. Little good the same Irish was to you and you looking for the start in Sparkhill. Shag all good it was to you when you wanted to order something to eat in an Italian café, afraid to look at the menu, that you wouldn't understand, no choice but to order "same here" like the others.

"Culture me arse," he said out loud. "Fuck culture. Fuck the Irish language. Are ye all half dead or what? Ye're as dull as fucking dishwater. I remember when there was life in this place. Sing us a song there, Peadar, in the name of Jaysus. Wake up this joint." He began to chant: "And down the glen came McAlpine's men, With their shovels slung behind them." He stopped, took a slug from his pint, and continued, to the wrong air:

"O mother dear, I'm over here,
Agus tá tusa thiar sa mbaile.
I'm over here, and *go deo arís*,
I'm never going back *abhaile*.
What keeps me here is the rake of beer,
The ladies—fair play *dóibh*—and the crack."

This last line was accompanied by the pumping of his fist up and down in the air, an action specifically sexual. "Up the Arsenal. Crumpet for the craw-thumpers."

"Sssssssh…" His brother was pulling at his sleeve. Shamey continued louder, "they wouldn't leave the Crown, with glasses flying and biddies crying, counters cracking and barmen jacking. Paddy was on the town. Paddy was on the tear."

"Sssssssh, *an sagart*, the priest."

"Honey Fitz," Shamey's brother was called, after the mother. Peadar Rua had christened her in the Kennedy Camelot days, because her tongue was so sweet, and so sharp.

"The priest?" Shamey surveyed the room with

drunken deliberation. "I must be blind drunk," he said to himself, "I don't see any priest." Then he spotted the young man that had thrown the shovel of soil on his father's coffin. A man with a powerful wrist, who held the shovel at full length, as if it were a spoon. There he sat like any man, collar open in his black shirt. "How's it goin', Padre?" Shamey proffered the hand that had such phallic connotations a few moments before. "How's she cuttin?" Tom Connor shook his hand. "Do you want to sit down?"

"What's that you're having?"

"Porter."

"You'll have a half-one?"

"No thanks."

"The priest that can't drink whiskey hasn't been born yet. Hi. Two pints and two Paddies. When you're ready," he added, seeing Collins, the barman, didn't look too happy. It was long after official closing time, but then there were no guards on the island so they kept their own times. Collins thought Shamey had more than enough already but what could he say when he was with the priest.

"What part are ye in?"

"The Brum, Birmingham."

"I knew Birmingham well a few years ago."

"What part?"

"All over, Solihull, Saltley, Sparkbrook, Sparkhill, Small Heath, Perry Barr, West Bromwich—I was at a few matches there, and in Villa Park as well."

"You know the Brum well."

"It's many's the day, and many a night I spent around Sparkhill."

"You did, like fuck. Isn't that where we are. How

long since you were there?"

"It's the best part of ten years. I spent most of my holidays there when I was a student."

"I never thought it was a place for holidays. Had you relations over there?"

"Working I used to be, not much of a holiday."

"You mean real work?—digging deep and throwing far back?"

"Hard work, pick and fork, shovel and jackhammer."

"Who were you with?"

"Kennedy mostly, a while with Baillie, a spell with Ruane."

"Kennedy, R.S., fucking K. It's a small world. I was a while with Kennedy myself, got lumped off about three months ago. The ould cunt of an agent wouldn't put me on overtime, so I reared up and put a few fucks in him, so he gave me my cards."

"If it was the same agent that was in it in my time, you were nobody unless you were from County Clare. Do they still pick up at the Black Horse?"

"You were over alright, *a mhac*. You'll have another drink?"

"I'll get this one."

"Come over here," Shamey called his brother. "Come over here and meet a man that worked in the Brum long before they heard of Honey Fitz over there."

As the night went on Tom Connor felt Shamey was getting more sober as he himself got drunker. Whiskey had never agreed with him after porter. He knew he would be sick before the night was out.

They talked of people and of places in Birmingham, the Antelope in Sparkhill, the Bear and the Mermaid, pubs that the Black Maria police "paddy wagons" had not been unknown to pull up outside. They talked about the legendary figures of the Irish diaspora, names like Elephant John, Pincher Mac, and Tiger Flynn. You would think they had known each other for years. Shamey's verdict at the end of the night was: "You'd never think you were a priest. You're like any man."

"I have to be off. I have mass in the morning."

Tom felt nausea rise within him—he was not able for the whiskey chaser. He hurried to the concrete outside toilet that stood open to the stars. He vomited all he had eaten and drunk, the undigested lumps tearing at his throat. The retching stopped and he leaned, sweating against the wall. There was vomit all over the floor. He threw grass in on top of it, and went home. He slept as soon as his head hit the pillow.

"Come on lads, and we'll knock a rise out of old Bridgie Hughie." It was Honey's idea. The younger men were gathered under the whitethorn bush beyond the pub, an hour after it closed. They had consumed a six-pack of Guinness and a bottle of poteen. Money was flush since the Fitzs came home. "What did you say we'd knock out of her?"

"We'll knock a rise out of her."

"Honey wants to ride ould Bridgie." There was a loud guffaw of laughter.

"Rise, I said. Jays, I'm not that badly off. I'd sooner go up on a clipped hedge than go up on Bridgie. Is anyone game for a bit of crack?"

"Can ye not leave an ould woman alone?" Paddy McEvilly said.

"Would ye listen to the saint? Listen to the holy angel. He would never knock a wall, or interfere with the council work on the roads. Paddy is a goody-goody. The fact that your brother-in-law has Biddie's grass wouldn't have anything to do with it? From what I hear, he mightn't have it for long."

"You'd be surprised," Paddy said.

"You were always the same, McEvilly," said Honey, "always causing trouble, never satisfied with anything."

"Who's causing trouble?"

"Forget it. You're a dry lot. There is no crack around here the way there used to be. We won't do her any harm, just give her a bit of a fright, for old times' sake."

"I'm with you," Jackie Reilly said, "for old times' sake. The bitch nearly murdered me with her blackthorn stick." They set off. Bridgie had no light, and there was no sound from inside as they crept around the house.

"Me-ow-ow-ow."

"Me-ow." Honey's attempt to imitate a cat was not as good as Jackie's. They had a laugh when they heard a cat answer them from a distance. "O, fuck." Honey hit his knee on the edge of a half-barrel of water, outside the back door. "Give us a hand, here."

"You're horsing it altogether now." Jackie knew that the house, built against the side of the hill, had a step down into the kitchen. Honey put his weight against the tub—half a wooden spray barrel. It overturned with a big splash. The water was held back for a moment by an old coat Bridgie used to keep out the draught but it was soon swept aside. The water swirled around the dark kitchen, washed the unraked ashes from the fireplace, swept around Bridgie's knees, where she had died, kneeling at the bedside, the top half of her body collapsed on the bed. She had died in prayer. "Isn't it a wonder she didn't start blinding," Jackie said as they headed home.

"Win or lose, we'll drink the booze."

Tom Connor awoke with a start, not recognising the voice or knowing where it came from. "We're the last generation anyways." He recognised it now, the voice of the man in whose house he was sleeping, Jack Phaddy. "Have you a match, Connor?" Jack was groping about in the dark. "Light the shagging candle until we have a talk."

"What's wrong? Is it only now you're coming home?"

"We're the last generation."

"Ssssh, or you'll waken the next generation."

"The likes of us will never be again. *'Ní bheidh ár leithéidí arís ann,'* as the old man of the Blaskets said it, something like that anyway."

"Maybe the world will be just as well off."

"I don't want to hear you talking like that, Connor." Jack managed to light the candle. He had a bottle of poteen under his arm. "This island wasn't a bad place to live at all, but it's dead now, and you and me are going to wake it tonight." He sat down on the edge of the bed. "Have a drop from the bottle. It'll put hair on your balls, if you have any."

"A priest wouldn't have any of them."

"Not fucking likely. Now that you did mention it, I met a priest once over in the village, in Tigh Sheoinín, that gombeen man ye have over there coining money in his shop and pub. A priest from the North, a nice man, no more than yourself. You wouldn't take him to be a priest, with a yellow shirt and blue trousers on him. We had a great chat. He told me a good one about a priest up in his own place, a man that had a child in every second house, a cuckoo in every nest. One of his mates made up a song and when they would meet, he'd start '*A shagairt na magarlach mór*,' 'O priest of the big bollocks.'"

"You were saying the island is on its last legs."

"Can't you see that yourself, all the young girls gone."

"There is not much for them here, at this time of the year anyway."

"There's plenty here for them. Isn't this place better than to be skivvying for some big noise in America, or living in a roomeen above in Dublin. A woman is her own boss here."

"I know one 'boss' that would prefer if her husband went to bed."

"There's more to marriage than the bed, Connor. I'll bet they didn't tell you that up in Maynooth."

"They didn't, or about the bed either."

"I'd say now that you would have a good idea of what to do with it."

"I know one thing. If I was a married man it's not in a priest's celibate bed I'd be at this time of the night."

"There isn't much thrashing a man can do when the barn is full. There isn't much crack in beating the sheaf up against the barn door."

"When will it be?"

"There's a long time yet. Do you know, Tom, I'm so happy. Thanks be to the great God. In all seriousness it's a shame that priests have to be deprived of creation. To feel a child moving, kicking in a woman's womb. To see the little pink bundle when it's born; then to see it growing up to be different, someone unique. Isn't it a wonderful thing."

"You have a great wife, God bless her."

"Mary is great. What other woman would put up with the likes of me?"

Jack went down to the kitchen and after a little while and a lot of noise, came back with two mugs of poteen punch.

"*Sláinte mhaith*, and if you're ever changed from here, I hope they send a man in your place that I will be able to talk to. You're a man where men are scarce, *fear, áit a bhfuil fir gann*."

"*Seafóid*, Bullshit."

"It's no *seafóid* at all. We might not agree with everything you try, with everything you say or do. Maybe you didn't get the support you deserved when you tried to set up the community council."

"It's easy for you to say that now. You weren't very complimentary about the same council down in the bar tonight."

"That isn't the place to be drawing down serious matters—on a Sunday night anyway. McEvilly is always doing his nut about something or other."

"If he is itself he's a good man. He has a bit of go in him. It's a pity there are not more like him."

"He always manages to put people against him. He won't achieve very much with that kind of attitude."

"It's time people here forgot the old enmities and began pulling together."

"If things are not gone too far…"

"You're an awful man to be putting in on the priest at this time of the night." Mary was standing barefoot in the doorway, an old coat pulled around her, her face reddened with sleep, looking lovely. Tom thought he had never seen her look so pretty or so young. He tended to forget she was younger than himself despite having six children. "Come in here until we see you. This is my girl, Connor, my big *peata*, the finest woman in Ireland."

"Yourself and your *plamás*. Let the priest go to sleep."

"Get yourself a cup and have a drop of this stuff."

"I will not. Someone in this house has to keep their head."

"She won't drink in front of the priest. Did you know, Father, *a mhac*, that one would drink the cross off an ass, so long as there was nobody looking at her."

"Don't believe a word he says, Father."

"Sit here beside me and make yourself comfortable. You'll always have it to say you were in bed with a priest."

"You're going too far now, Jack."

"If I was an Eskimo I'd give her to you for the night, on loan. Did you know an Eskimo—I think it's an Eskimo—gives the loan of his wife to any man that comes visiting?"

"If that was true, we would all be on the missions to the Eskimos," Tom said. "A bishop in that country wouldn't have much trouble getting his priests to visit the houses."

"Ye mightn't be in any hurry visiting the old people."

"That's my girl. If I said something like that, she'd have my life."

"Leave her alone now. You're making her blush."

"Blush? Sure that one has no shame in her." The poteen was really going to his head now. "Do you not see where she's looking. She's trying to make out if the priest has anything between his legs.

For he's got no fallurum,
He's lost his dingdurum…"

"Can you not think of anything but dirt?"

"I know what I'm talking about. I know a woman is only interested in the one thing…Do you see that cross, Connor, the cross of Christ hanging there on the wall?"

"I do, of course. Why?"

"When a woman looks at that she's trying to make out what's inside that cloth that's tied around him. That's the only God she's interested in."

"Give over, Jack. Such an insult to Our Lord."

"And to every woman that ever lived," Tom Connor said quietly.

"That poteen is rising in your head," Mary said.

"I know what I'm talking about."

"You know everything except to have respect."

"I know."

"You know all right. That's all we ever hear, I, I, I. Go to bed and have a bit of sense. I'm sorry, Father."

"If we don't know each other well enough by now…"

"Sure we have to have the crack. We only live a while. I was only trying to rise Connor, to vex him, to see what kind of mettle he's made of…Goodnight, Tom."

He bent and kissed the priest on the mouth as he would a child.

"Sure we have to have the bit of crack. We're the last generation."

Tom Connor had a roaring hangover headache as he said mass the following morning. He was hoarse: his throat was sore from the vomiting the previous night.

The gospel of the mass was direct Marcan talk—better to have a millstone hung about your neck and be drowned in the depth of the sea, than to scandalise Christ's little ones. As he read he wondered what the pious women in front of him would have thought of his being sick with drink the night before. He had an excuse, of course—was it not for the sake of the Kingdom he drank, to get the courage to get to know his parishoners better. Did the Lord leave the revellers at the wedding of Cana drinking water? Any excuse.

He remembered something else about millstones— about the mills of God grinding slowly. He felt they must be all ringing inside his head.

It was a pet day. The wind had gone south, a little west of south. It was mild and dry. The forecast was bad, rain followed by gales. The sea looked calm still. He would have to get back to the mainland before the storm. He visited the school on the way to the slip.

It was easy to see from the school that the island population was dwindling fast. Fifteen children, from four families, in a corner of a big classroom, the other rooms idle, schoolrooms that once catered for nearly a hundred children.

The teacher was past pension age but she acted as a substitute while the school management board sought a replacement. Despite a national surplus of teachers they had so far failed to fill the position. Tom felt it sad that it seemed to be for emigration the children were being schooled. They would leave for secondary school at twelve, and as far as the island was concerned that was probably the end of them. There would be some on holiday from time to time, but as far as the long-term was concerned...

His mood of depression deepened when on his way down to the sea he noticed walls knocked here and there. He knew that he should not let things like that depress him but they hurt him deeply. There was some turmoil going on, some row with its roots in trouble over seaweed rights a hundred years before, maybe. The cause of the trouble was long forgotten, but as with the civil war on the national scene, people still took sides with the people they always took sides with. Meetings split on expected lines, whatever the topic. Things would be quiet for a long time but the old enmities continued to simmer beneath the surface.

It was easy to rebuild a wall, but who would be satisfied with that? Revenge would have to be exacted, maybe on the wrong person. Young fellows sometimes knocked walls for the fun of the fight it would spawn. At a meeting to try and sort things out, someone would take umbrage, walk out, claim there was favouritism. What was it really but national and international politics in minuscule. Tom often felt that the major diplomats on the world stage should be brought to the island to learn their trade. If only people's energy could be directed in a positive way...

It was Patcheen John's turn. He was a small, broad, swarthy man, married to Martha McEvilly. Only two of the islanders went across as the day was fine, Paddy McEvilly on the engine, Patcheen on the seat nearest the prow, smoking his pipe.

Tom saw nobody from the time he left the shore until he reached the presbytery. The end of the world could have come and gone, he thought, unknown to them on the island.

Marion welcomed him home with a kiss and a plate of stew. She looked well in a long red skirt and black blouse, her hair tied up in gypsy fashion. There was a lovely fire, and the house smelled so clean. "So much for celibacy," Tom said, a hot potato in his mouth.

"What was that?"

"It's so nice to be home again, to have someone nice to make me welcome."

"It's nice to have a man come back from his conquests."

"Everything is nice so."

"I missed you. The place was cold without you."

"I was gone only one night."

The evening passed in pleasant banter. Tom looked forward to having evening mass over so that he could relax. The hangover and the sea crossing left him longing for a good night's sleep.

Teresa Phádraic Mhichilín had gone for a walk about three o'clock after having a cup of tea. On short winter days she liked to walk out along the cliff-top where the wind would catch her hair and make it flow free.

Teresa was mentally handicapped, what people called "simple." All her brothers and sisters were away working in England or America, except Barbara who was at boarding-school in the city. Teresa could cook and sew and look after herself in most ways. She had very little speech, a kind of moaning which only her mother really understood.

She was a good-looking girl who dressed well in the fashionable clothes her sisters sent home. Some of the young men at the door of the chapel on Sunday would nudge each other approvingly as she passed in with her mother. This worried Pádraic and Cáit, human nature being what it is.

They worried that Monday evening when she was not back at five o'clock. It would soon be dark. Pádraic walked to the top of the hillock but could not see her anywhere. He thought she might have gone in to mass. There would be one at five if the priest had got back.

"You would think," he said to Cáit when he returned to the house, "she would come home first as she always did. I'll go up to the chapel and see is there any sign of her."

No sign. He went into the priest to make enquiries. He was putting on his vestments. "I'm sure she will be home, Pádraic, by the time you are home yourself. Let me know if she's not."

"You'll say a prayer."

"Of course I will. I'll call into the house after mass. I'm sure she will be back by then, with the help of God."

She was not. Cáit's face was white with worry.

"Come with me in the car, Pádraic. We'll drive around the roads. She must have walked further than she intended and the darkness caught up with her. Don't worry, Cáit, we'll have her back with us."

He was beginning to doubt it himself.

They stopped the battered mini outside Tigh Sheoinín, the village pub. "Tell the lads to be ready," he said to Tom Jennings, the old man who owned the place. "Tell them to have torches, lanterns, ropes in case."

"We'll have everything ready, Father."

Tom was certain he would, even though he and old Tom did not see eye to eye on many matters. But in a case like this all was forgotten except the poor person in trouble. He and Pádraic searched the roads as far as she could have possibly walked. They did not have much hope of finding her.

"She used often go out on the cliffs," Pádraic said.

"Do you think she went there today?"

"That's what I'm afraid of. What chance would she have of coming safe from the cliff in the dark?"

"If she is up there often, she knows the place well."

"You know she tried to kill herself before?"

"I didn't know. How long ago is that?"

"Three or four years ago. The nurse was visiting one night. She was telling of a friend of hers that had cut her wrists. Didn't Teresa try the same thing the next day. And you would think she was taking no notice of what the nurse said. Thanks be to God she cut the wrong place. The marks are still there."

"What kind of form was she in today, Pádraic?"

"Good enough form. She was in good form the other time too. The poor girl hasn't much sense."

There were men gathered at the gable of the thatched house when they returned. There were five or six others on the road, everyone ready and anxious to help in time of trouble.

Women and children were gathered in the big kitchen. A little boy was pushed to the forefront. He stood chewing his thumb, a shamed look on his face. His secret was in danger of being revealed—he had spent the day mitching in the old castle.

"I saw her this evening, Father."

"What time was that, Ginger?"

"About the time school is over."

"You're a big liar, Ginger Fahy. You were not at

school at all today."

"Let him be. Where exactly did you see her?"

"Up by the old castle, out towards the cliffs, the way she is always going."

"The dog, Pádraic." Someone had a brain-wave. "Isn't that black and white dog always with her."

"That ould dog is dead." He didn't like to say that he had drowned it, thrown it in from the cliff. There were rumours that it used be after sheep at night. Pádraic had no proof but when he tried to keep him in, he had barked all night. He would be in serious trouble if he was found to be worrying sheep. Mick Macken had promised him a pup for Teresa.

The search began. When they got to the cliff-top the men fanned out into a line in the great waste of crag. They stood about ten feet apart from each other, each carrying a light. They walked carefully on the broken stones. It was so easy to break a leg there. They called out Teresa's name again and again, in case the lights would scare her. They knew at the same time that the shouting might scare her too but what else could they do?

The wind which had been whispering in from the sea was beginning to strengthen, to come in short gusts, outriders of the storm that was marshalling its forces out there in the Atlantic. The sea thumped a rhythmic dead beat against the base of the cliff. What would the people out on the island think if they could see lights where they had never seen them before? Fairies? Magic?

"What is that?" Big Mick Macken was the first to hear it. He blessed himself. Then they all heard it, a high-pitched, heartrending kind of scream. A banshee?

Then a light picked it out, a ragged kid goat, its leg stuck in a split of the crag, its companions scattered by the lights and the shouting. The foot was bruised badly. Mick tied a handkerchief around it, and put the goat under his jacket, where the thumping of its heart soon slowed in the warmth of his body.

After five hours of searching, shouting and scrambling over broken stones, they had found nothing. A thick squally wetting drizzle was being driven in the strengthening gale. Visibility was reduced to almost nothing. Batteries were wearing out, lights fading. They reluctantly decided that nothing more could be done until morning. Everyone seemed to have suddenly given up hope. For Padraic's sake they talked of her maybe sheltering somewhere, or gone home by a different way, perhaps.

The women were saying the rosary when they got back. The men got quietly to their knees, steam rising from their wet clothes in the heat of the kitchen. There was a note of resignation in the prayer, a "welcome be the will of God." There was a feeling too that it was for consolation for Teresa's family they prayed.

When the prayers were said the women busied themselves preparing tea. Some of the men went home to change their clothes. The others waited to help carry Cáit and Pádraic through the night. It was like a wake, only worse. The uncertainty left people impatient. The element of hope gnawed at the nerves.

Cáit had married Pádraic a couple of months before her seventeenth birthday. They had twelve children, two of whom had died at birth. Although her hair was completely white, she was still a beautiful woman. The nervousness which had given her face a pinched look earlier in the evening was gone. She was satisfied that now, one way or the other, all was in the hands of God. All that could be done had been done. All they could do now was wait for Teresa or until her body was found.

"We'll find her in the morning, with the help of God. As soon as it's daylight we will be out again." Mick Macken was shamefaced about sitting about while there was searching to be done. The little goat he had found lay under his chair, the wounded leg cleaned and wrapped in a cloth.

"We shouldn't have let her out on the cliffs at all," Pádraic said, self-accusingly.

"Sure it's nobody's fault. She liked to go out there, and nothing ever happened before."

"We have to accept the will of God."

"That's life."

"Isn't it happy for her. Didn't we often hear that it's the likes of her that's nearest to God."

"Teresa is a saint if there ever was one."

"As innocent as the day she was born."

"The old people used to say that it's to the people he loves best that God gives the biggest crosses."

"We don't know the day or the hour."

The silence was broken from time to time with such statements. The women especially were impatient, their hands unused to being idle. Most of the men smoked pipes. They sat looking steadily at the fire. The wind, blowing in the chimney, took on a higher whistling note and drew tongues of blue and purple flame from the dark brown turf.

"The fair was not much good the last day."

"It was not, but if the radio has it right, they're

going up a bit."

"Those marts must be a good idea. It's a nice clean way to sell cattle. You'd get the price according to their weight, anyhow."

"It isn't much of a farmer that can't tell the weight of a beast by looking at it."

"There must be big farmers up your side of the country, Father. There must be plenty of money there— all the priests that come out of it."

"If there was money in it, would we be coming down here collecting from ye. Sure I wouldn't be in this job at all if I was able to do anything else."

"Joking us you are now. Whatever brought you into the priesthood, it wasn't that."

"There was a priest up our way once that used be often talking about how much it cost his parents to make a priest out of him. One Sunday morning he went through all the figures of how much it cost. On the way out of the chapel a man was heard saying to his neighbour: 'A cheaper priest would have done us.'"

"It must cost a fair bit all the same."

"It doesn't cost a penny if you don't have it."

They spent a good while looking into the fire in silence. Rain was lashing the window. Big drops fell down the chimney and spluttered on the fire.

"Which of the two places do you prefer, Father, here or the island?"

"When I'm here I say I prefer the village. When I'm on the island I say the opposite. I have to keep the two sides with me."

"Sure priests don't tell lies."

"Maybe it's no lie, that I'm the sort of person that is satisfied wherever he is."

"A good way to be."

"That isn't completely true either, I suppose. I was not very happy stuck in the college before I came here."

"We're badly enough off here, but at least we have the road. You would pity the island people cut off so often by the sea."

"Aren't they the strange crowd too, Father." Mick Macken said, "the way they kept up the Irish."

Someone else added from the corner, "Without the few shillings from the government, I don't think there would be many of them speaking it."

"Isn't everyone free," Tom said, "to speak whatever language they like. Isn't the Irish our own."

"It's not much good to you in Camden Town."

"What weight is it either? Haven't the other nationalities their own languages, the Italians, the Pakistanis, the Indians."

"It's not the same at all. The Paddy is in a bad way over there if he hasn't English. You would expect the foreigners to have their own languages."

"Are we not trying to show for seven hundred years that we're foreigners too? Anyway there are not many in the Gaeltacht now that are not bilingual. They can speak English and Irish."

"It's often said that it's English the people of the Gaeltacht are teaching their children."

"I hear that said, even about Connemara. But if the people in the place want to change their language, what is there to stop them?"

"If Connemara doesn't keep the Irish, it's well to kiss it goodbye."

"I don't know," the priest said. "Maybe there isn't

much change of reviving Irish until the Gaeltacht itself dies out."

"Sure there would be no right Irish left at all then."

"It wouldn't be the same, I know, but I'm afraid the revival won't come until we see the end of the Gaeltacht as we know it."

"You think people won't really worry about it until it's almost died out."

"And that itself mightn't worry the people of Ireland. But as long as the Gaeltacht is there as a kind of museum the nation is satisfied, and there is not much chance of a revival."

The crow of the cock cut across the conversation. Suddenly everyone remembered what had them there. Their tiredness, the warmth of the house, and the conversation had lulled them into a kind of comfortable timelessness. Chairs creaked and feet shuffled. Pádraic Mhichilín stood at the back door and listened. A barking dog answered the crow of the cock in the still black night.

"We won't feel the daylight coming now."

"We'll make a cup of tea, so that you'll be ready to go out as soon as it's bright." The women were delighted to have something to do.

They were drinking the tea when a noise was heard outside. The door opened in. Teresa stood there, drenched wet, her long hair stuck to her head and face with the rain. She had only one shoe. Her other ankle was stained with blood. She had the body of the black and white sheepdog in her arms. She smiled. She carried the body of the dog and laid it on the mat at the door of her room. Its eyes had been picked out, and the bare bone showed in the skull.

"Come down to the fire, Teresa, *a ghrá*. You're drowned. You'll have to change your clothes." Her mother wanted to throw her arms around her and kiss her, but she knew Teresa did not like public displays of affection. She was already on her knees, caressing the kid goat.

"Thanks be to God," people were saying, "Isn't it great to be alive."

"Do you think she'll have to be put in a home now?" Pádraic asked the priest at the gate, as the last of the neighbours headed home.

"Why would you? Sure Teresa would be lost in a hospital, lost without yourself and Cáit. Don't blame yourself for what happened tonight. You can't be always watching her and in a way it might be a good thing. It showed she was well able to make out for herself."

Tom Connor was dreaming. It was during mass. His server would not stop ringing the little bell. "Sssssh," Tom hissed through his teeth. He would not stop.

"I'll get it." It was Marion's voice that awoke him. The phone was ringing.

"Let it ring," Tom said. "They'll ring back if it's anything important. Everyone in the place knows I was out all night."

He answered the phone when the ringing refused to stop. The call was from the island post office. Could he be at the landing place in half an hour. There was a currach going over for him to anoint Bridgie Hughie. "Is she bad?" He looked at his watch. It was only half past nine. The tiredness dragged at his body. "She couldn't be any worse."

He had a good idea she was already dead but that

they didn't like to say so—probably a question of when the soul departs the body. The angel of death had not been outdone the night before after all. It would be a release for Bridgie—wasn't it nice to think of her being in heaven for Christmas.

Marion had breakfast ready by the time he finished on the phone. He gulped down the tea and toast, put on his oilskins and wellington boots, and set out west towards the sea.

It seemed that no one had got out of bed yet after the search—there was nobody to be seen. The sea looked very wild, the south-west wind driving big rolling waves diagonally onto the beach. "No currach will go out in that gale," he said to himself. He had never seen seas like them. He hoped the island men would have more sense than to attempt the crossing. It took a lot of faith to put four lives in danger for the sake of anointing an old woman who was almost certainly without sin.

Fifty yards from the shore his oilskins were already wet with flying spray. The wind howled menacingly through the stone walls. A black cloud hung over the island. If that shower, and the squall of wind that would inevitably come with it, caught a currach on the sea it would almost certainly founder. But there was no currach to be seen.

"They must be out of their minds." Mick Macken was suddenly standing beside him, accompanied by some more men from the village. Then Tom saw it, the prow of the currach rising from the waves. It looked like a rocket in the distance. Then the transom was to be seen, sliding down another wave. Out of sight for a moment, it seemed to be facing towards the island when it next came into view.

"They're going home, thanks be to God," someone said. "They'll have shelter going ashore behind there. They wouldn't have a hope here." They were soon facing the mainland again, having gone out towards the south-west the better to judge their run towards the beach. They would have to time it perfectly if they were to survive—given the speed and the break of the waves.

More and more people were coming from the village, in awe and admiration of men who would face the sea on such a day. Tom's own admiration was somewhat dampened by the knowledge that he would have to go out there with them. At the same time there was more satisfaction to be had from it than from searching for Teresa in the previous night's darkness. Here was something that was easier to come to grips with, the age-old struggle of man against the sea, and it all for the love of God, skills of centuries on the oars against the power and treachery of the sea. It would not be their fault if Bridgie was not pitchforked in across the gates of Heaven. But it was no more than what they would themselves expect from others in the hour of need.

"That's Tomás Mháire Dhubh in the front," someone said with the respect and admiration due to a legendary seaman.

"And Patcheen John..."

"And Jack Phaddy."

They all knew that there was at least a truce in the long-running feud between the last two, for the sake of putting the best crew in the island on the sea. Both were related to Bridgie but it was to Patcheen she had signed the land.

Twice they approached and rowed away again when they saw the danger of being carried too far to the north. The shower could now be seen to sweep across from the island. If they did not make a landing on their third attempt they would be in serious trouble but no one better understood the danger than the three men in the currach. They came ashore exactly at the right point. Up to twenty men waded in to grab the little boat and carry it out of the backwash.

"We had no bother at all." Jack Phaddy was dismissive of the wonder and congratulations of the mainlanders. He delighted in giving the impression that it was no more than a routine exercise for the men of the island but all three were proud and happy men, full of confidence for the return journey. This day would be remembered as long as stories would be told.

"Ye had better shelter from the shower." Rain and hailstones lashed them. The sea looked like a boiling cauldron. People sheltered under upturned currachs and behind walls. The shower had blown over in minutes. "Ye'll have it tough against the wind."

"The engine will do some of the work for us. We have it in the bottom of the currach."

When the sea had calmed a little after the shower they pushed down the currach again. The men of the village gave it a great shove and scampered back from the waves. The three oarsmen rowed hard. The prow of the currach leaped into the incoming waves and broke through with a loud bang into the troughs behind them. Patcheen and the priest changed places quickly, Patcheen getting the engine started as soon as he reached the stern. The other two continued to row, Tom Connor bailing out the splashing spray from the bottom of the currach with an old saucepan.

The rows of waves, as high as two-storey houses, scared Tom. In the shallows between the waves it looked as if each oncoming wave would swamp them but it was for such waves the currach was designed. Again and again the frail basin of laths and canvas mounted the great swells, wobbled for a moment on top and slid down in preparation for the next one. An image formed in the mind of the priest—inspired by the shape of the currach—an image of the shoe of Christ as he walked on the water.

For a long time they rowed directly south-west meeting the waves head on. They then gradually moved west, making little headway, as they had to swing around the currach again and again to face some of the more dangerous waves. It was a fight for survival now and even the priest had forgotten his fear. Every wave successfully faced was a new achievement. They lost count of time, rowing, bailing, manning the little Seagull outboard. Things got easier in the shelter of the island and they had relatively little trouble going ashore on the slipway.

When Tom reached the west, Bridgie was still in the position in which she had died. Rigor mortis had set in while she was in a kneeling position. They laid her out on her side on the narrow bed. "The way she has the legs, you would think..." Jack Phaddy remembered where he was in time to stop in mid-sentence. Laughter at the incongruity of it all exploded inside him. To cover up he snorted into his handkerchief. Patcheen John thought he was crying or pretending to be. Bridgie's land had been signed to himself and he did not like to see anyone grieving more than he did for the old woman.

"Isn't it you that's taking it bad." Jack gave a grunt, and changed the subject. "Is there any way of straightening her out?"

"I can pull the legs if you press down on the knees."

"I don't think we'll do any good. Sure St Peter won't be long straightening her out."

"Lord have mercy on her poor soul, do you realise what you're saying?"

"Don't worry, Patcheen. Even if she's able to hear me itself, I don't think she will be able to come back and take the biteen of land with her."

"If we were anywhere but the corpse house…"

"Come on," said Jack, "until we make the coffin. It won't be so noticeable when she is in the box."

Tom Connor helped Martha Patcheen to wash Bridgie's body. They failed to get the mixture of coal dust and snuff off the tops of her fingers, but camouflaged them with a rosary beads. Tom went straight to bed as soon as he got back to Jack Phaddy's, his digs.

Some would have said that Bridgie Hughie hadn't a friend in the world. She had not encouraged familiarity but that did not prevent her from having a good wake. A half-barrel of Guinness was brought up from the bar, tobacco and cigarettes placed loosely on plates on the table and little window-sills. Children gathered stools and chairs from the nearest houses. Only necessary work, like milking and the preparation of meals, was done until after a burial. There was hammering and sawing in the yard of the house as the coffin was shaped from white deal boards. Inside the rosary had been said. The talk was beginning.

"Peadar Rua said he heard the banshee when he got home from the pub Sunday night."

"No wonder he heard something strange, the way he was throwing back the drink."

"They say a lot of people heard noise that night."

"And there were lights across on the cliffs last night."

"I wouldn't be too sure about the banshee. A couple of cats courting."

"It was a quare cat, I'm telling you," said Peadar Rua. "I didn't hear a screech like it since the day I was born and that's more than four score years ago."

"Maybe it was that cat with no tail Bríd Nóra brought home last year from the Isle of Man."

"I'd say there was more than the tail cut," Jack Phaddy said. "I suppose you often heard of a 'cut cat,' Peadar. He has a higher-pitched voice than a tom. It's like that choir they have in Rome."

"What has Rome to do with a cut cat?"

"Did you never hear of that choir in Rome that you have to be squeezed before you get into it? Only bullocks need apply."

"Tell us another one."

"It's true. It keeps the voice from breaking. Sure there are no women allowed into the Vatican."

"The Lord almighty save us. Do you hear the talk of him in the house of the dead."

"We all know that it was two-legged cats were screeching that night. And it would be no harm to cut some of them." Paddy McEvilly spoke angrily.

"And what's got into our Paddy now?" Jackie Reilly asked in a contemptuous voice.

"As if you don't know. The doctor and police should have been brought here before that old lady was laid out."

"Didn't the priest see her?"

"What does the priest know about it? Can he prove that she wasn't murdered?"

"Murder." There was a moment's silence, not just in the kitchen where the men were but in the bedroom, where Bridgie's body was laid out, with the women sitting around it. No one wanted to miss the excitement. "All I know," Paddy McEvilly started again, "is that two people that are here left the *sceach gheal* Sunday night to knock a 'rise,' as they called it, out of old Bridgie. There's nothing more heard of her until she's found dead. All I'm saying is that the guards should be asked to investigate."

"The right one that's looking for the guards, the very one that gave them hell when they were on the island looking for dog licences and poteen."

"Isn't that exactly what I was saying at the time. They're nowhere to be found when they are really needed."

"You don't need to be making Agatha Christie out of yourself at all, McEvilly," Jack Phaddy said. "We all know that Bridgie died of the old age. Why can't we have a bit of crack and conversation without you coming up with one of your ridiculous theories?"

"There is nothing ridiculous about looking for a bit of justice for an old woman."

"I'll tell you exactly what did happen on Sunday night." Jackie Reilly was roused. "Maybe it will shut your big mouth. Shamey and myself went back and let a couple of screeches like two cats outside Bridgie's. We didn't see a thing or hear a thing or lay a hand on the old woman. I don't care what guards or doctors or priests come around the place. That's the truth. That's what happened. And if that doesn't shut your mouth, McEvilly, I know what will."

"And what's that?"

"I'll shut your fucking mouth for you if you come outside."

"Will ye for God's sake have sense and a bit of respect for the dead."

"If the people that got the land and were supposed to be looking after her, were taking much care of her, she wouldn't have died as she did. They're the ones that have to take the blame. We didn't do anything. If he's not afraid to come outside, I'll show him how to shut his face."

"Outside so, and we'll have fair play in the yard."

"Don't say that you're going fighting outside the dead-house." But the young men were going out the door.

"Surely you're not going with them," Peadar Rua said to Jack Phaddy. But he followed the younger men. "*Is fearr an troid ná an t-uaigneas*—the fight is better than the loneliness," he said.

Jackie was a couple of inches taller than Paddy. He knew from spadework and wall building that he was strong. He quite liked Paddy and admired his courage in speaking out. At the same time he hoped to beat him and earn respect for himself.

Neither of them was much good at fighting. They tried to do too much and ended up wrestling more than boxing. They broke away from each other, stood back, circled like two cockerels. Then Paddy fell. Shamey Fritz had tripped him.

"Bastards. You said there would be fair play."

McEvilly rose, a stone in his hand. "If you want to play it rough…" Patcheen John, his brother-in-law, caught his arms from behind before he could throw the stone.

"Break it up lads, for Christ's sake." The priest stood between the fighting men, awakened from his sleep by someone beating at his window and shouting, "They're killing each other up at the corpse house."

"Stay out of this, Connor," Paddy McEvilly roared. "You can do your business—you can anoint the bastard when I have him killed."

"You wouldn't kill a mouse." Reilly attacked him again. McEvilly hadn't a chance because his arms were held. He was hit directly on the nose. Tom Connor, trying to keep them apart, got a stray fist in the eye. Then it was free for all over the yard. The older men tried to break it up without success.

Then there was a screech, and another, the shock of scalding water, and the fight was over. Jack Phaddy had a torch in one hand, a kettle in the other. "If ye don't take heed of the priest ye'll have to take heed of me. I'll scald the balls off the next man to throw a punch. Have a bit of sense, ye amadáns, and have a little respect for the dead."

The young men's anger cooled as quickly as it had flared. People drifted back into the house. "The Lord have mercy on ould Bridgie," said Peadar Rua, "Isn't it she that would have enjoyed that. She was a great one for a fight in life and devil the stopping her in death."

Bridgie's light body in its home-made white coffin was brought to the chapel that next evening and left before the altar for the night. She was buried in the little rocky graveyard after morning mass. Three browned skulls and the other bones that had been disturbed in the grave-making were placed reverently beside her coffin, bones of those that had begotten her to be the last of generations that tore a living from rock and sea.

The priest's eye was black and swollen as he threw a shovelful of soil on the white-sheeted coffin. "Dust thou art and into dust thou shalt return but the Lord will raise you up on the last day."

People stood momentarily in silent prayer at their own family graves, then went home.

Like the calm that follows a storm, Tom Connor found himself with nothing to do except say daily mass, a sharp contrast to the week's turbulent start. He spent the time doing little jobs around the house, sharing the cooking and cleaning chores with Marion, sleeping as much as he could. He believed strongly in sleeping and relaxation at such times in order to have strength in reserve to carry him through times of stress and trouble.

Marion was restless. She rushed about, washing, ironing, sweeping, cooking, mopping floors over and over again. She was worried. Her breasts and nipples were harder than usual. There was a kind of tickly tingling in them, like that time she had become pregnant. She couldn't be…How could she? They had taken precautions. She had gone on the pill when they had begun to sleep together first. It had not agreed with her. She had felt weak, inclined to fall. Then there were all those scares about heart trouble, veins. They had sent for condoms by post, answering an advertisement in a Sunday paper. They were awkward, but better than nothing. Could one have burst?

Why hadn't she kept a record of her last period?

Maybe there was nothing to worry about. The next one—if it came—would be no curse, more of a blessing, "*an t-ádh dearg*, the red luck."

She couldn't tell Tom she was worried. It would kill him. She would have to go away. She couldn't give another child up to strangers. As for abortion—the cure was worse than the disease.

She would get rid of herself. Jump in off the cliff. She knew she couldn't. Everlasting Hell would be worse than hell on earth. She had not much time for religion in many ways but she believed in a God that could be vindictive. He had to be. He had never done much for her, showed her much love.

Why had it to happen now? She had been happy. Why had they not left things as they were, left well alone? "Sex fucks up love," she said to herself, "outside marriage, at least." Would Tom be happy outside the priesthood? She couldn't ask him to give that up. His vocation meant so much to him. And how the people loved him!

She wouldn't tell him. At the same time she knew she would have to. She would need his advice, his help. And wouldn't it be his child too? How could she kill his child? The nicest and gentlest man she had ever met. Or was he? Was he the same as the rest of them?

But what was she worrying about? The pill always mucked up periods. That must be it, with the help of God, with Jesus's help. What could she do but be patient? Why did everything she did turn to shit? There must be a curse on her.

Could she not keep the child, rear it herself? Get work somewhere. The child would give her a reason for living. They would kill her at home if they knew. They had never known anything about England. It would kill them now that they had the family reared, them all fixed up, a daughter a school-teacher, getting on well together...

She asked Tom. "Could you ever see yourself being anything else but a priest?"

"Why do you ask?"

"No reason. Something to say."

"I don't think I would be able to do anything else at this stage of my life. Doesn't the collar suit me anyway, like an ass looking over a whitewashed wall?"

"Be serious, Tom. I'm not an imbecile."

"I suppose I'd like to be a farmer, though there isn't much profit in the farming at the moment."

"Wouldn't you be qualified to teach?"

"I taught a little in the college, but it was mainly in the study-hall I was, something half-way between a nurse and a prison guard. Of course they wouldn't get anyone other than a priest to do the likes of it for love or money. An obedient priest just had to do what the bishop said."

"You, obedient."

"Am I not obedient to you?"

"Sure. What kind of work would you like?"

"The type of work that most appealed to me was the kind of work I did in England as a student, pick and shovel. I often think when I'm doing the garden that I'm more at home behind the shovel than behind the altar."

After a while Marion asked: "Do you really mean it when you say you love me?"

"Of course I do. Why do you ask?"

"No why. It's just that I like to hear you say it. That's all."

Eight currachs crossed over from the island on Christmas Eve. Two buses had come from the city, full of people home from England and from America, students from secondary schools, as well as a few people who had gone to the city a few days previously to do the Christmas shopping.

There was wild excitement in Tigh Sheoinín, Jennings's shop-cum-pub. *Sean-nós* and modern songs and ballads, the sweet music of violin, accordeon and *bodhrán*, set and single dancing. Latest city fashions mixed easily with homespun tweeds and red petticoats. There was much excited talk in Irish and in English.

Night was falling as the currachs were launched but there was a great frosty full moon, a starry sky and calm sea. In living memory Christmas Eve weather had not been too bad to allow people home for the festival. The sound of the oars and the singing could be heard on the island long before any currach could be seen. Maybe Santa Claus would be in one of the currachs. Not likely, though. He was too cute. And anyway hadn't he his own sleigh. He didn't need a boat. No matter how much you tried to stay awake to see him, he always managed to slip in when your eyes drowsily closed.

By the time the currachs came ashore, the children had forgotten Santa Claus in the excitement of trying to find out "what has mammy?" There were turkeys and chocolates, lemonade and long red candles. There were cards and letters from Chicago, from Boston, Manchester, Birmingham, Huddersfield, Cardiff, Glasgow and London. It was the one day of the year you could say that emigration was worthwhile. People had to go away to come back and celebrate like this.

The island pub closed early—not because of the law

of the land; there was not much notice taken of that—but because it was considered a night to stay at home with the family. The pub opened specially for a couple of hours after midnight mass, with drinks stood by the pub owner, according to local custom. Needless to say there was seldom less than a full house. But that would come later.

Candles were lighted in every window and on every supper table. Like most of the houses Jack Phaddy's had a traditional evening meal, the giblets of a turkey, with Christmas cake to follow. A big red candle was lit before the meal. Prayers were said for the living and the dead. Before they sat down Jack broke a lighted sod of turf in the hearth. This was known as "breaking the devil's back." Jack called the devil a few names that would frighten even him.

The meal was over and the children getting ready for bed when there was a loud knock at the door. The latch was raised and a man with a long white beard, dressed in what looked like a red bedspread, entered. The children believed in Santa Claus just as they believed in God but they had never really expected to see either in their own kitchen.

"God bless all there."

"And the blessing of God on your good self," Jack said. "Would you be looking for somebody? It's late you're out on Christmas night."

"The only thing I'm looking for is children."

"Well, you can't have any of ours. We need them ourselves."

"It's not that I want to take them with me. I'd just like to talk to them for a little while."

"I don't know what sort of a man you are. If it's digs

you're looking for, I'm afraid you're out of luck. The priest has the only spare bed in the house."

"Daddy, daddy..." The children thought their father very thick. Little Máire had a word in his ear, as Santa Claus turned towards the door, and said, "Well, if there is no welcome for me..."

"It's *Deaidí na Nollag*, Father Christmas, Santa Claus, Dad. He has toys in his suitcase..."

"Don't tell me it's yourself that's in it. *Céad míle fáilte.*" Jack took Santa's hand and squeezed as hard as he could. "I never thought I'd have the pleasure."

"Fuck you, Jack," said Jackie Reilly into the false beard, his fingers squeezed and painful. He thought of his own plan for a bit of playful revenge. "Would there be any chance, man of the house, that you'd have a dropeen of whiskey for me. I'm frozen with the cold driving that deer in the frosty night. I thought the North Pole cold, but this is the worst night I was ever out." He opened the case. "Here you are, children. Your names are on your parcels." He sat back to drink the whiskey. "He has a suitcase just like the one that's under mammy and daddy's bed," said seven-year-old Seán.

Santa Claus rose to go when he had finished his whiskey. He took the bottle from the table. "This will keep me warm on the journey home to Mammy Christmas," Jackie said. "Sure you don't mind, man of the house. You have no taste for whiskey yourself."

"Only this time of the year," said Jack. "It's Christmas, all the same."

"You couldn't refuse poor Santa." Mary was enjoying the fun.

"I wouldn't mind you taking the bottle at all, except

that I have a cold."

"Take two aspirins and go to your bed early. I'm a long time travelling the roads of life, and I have learned that much."

Jack played his last card. "Sure I'll have to give a drink to the priest when he comes in from confession."

"Never mind the priest. He doesn't have to go to the North Pole."

"Let poor Santa have it," Mary said. "Let poor Santa…" The children had the last word.

There was always a special atmosphere at midnight mass on Christmas Eve. Candlelight in the darkness, hymns, joy mixed with loneliness in people's hearts. Thoughts were of youth, the loved ones Christmases had been shared with, now dead. Thoughts of Almighty God as a child in the manger.

In his sermon Tom Connor referred to the fact that he had spent much of the day in the confession box between island and village. It was not telling any confessional secret to say that he had heard many people say how sorry they were for having hurt neighbours in word or deed. They told God and they told the priest that they were sorry. It was a pity the hurt neighbour could not hear that expression of sorrow. How many people did not speak for years, afraid to look at one another, unaware of the other's forgiveness? He believed that people's regret was genuine and that they wanted to make a new start. He would call a meeting in the new year to see what they could do for the island's future if people were prepared to pull together and forget past differences.

Tom was rowed across to the mainland at two in the

morning. He would have mass in the village at midday. Island and mainland alternated year after year with midday and midnight masses.

Marion and Tom sat before the fire for a long time that night, having a drink together. From time to time they were lost in their own thoughts, musing on times past. They had in mind taking a few days' break after Christmas to visit their own relations. Tom had not seen his aunt or uncle for a long time. They now lived in a bungalow in a town, having sold the land as they got too old to manage it, and it was clear that Tom was not going to work it. Selling the land had cut him to the quick, despite the fact that he had set his face on a different road. It was hard to let it go just a couple of generations after having been won from the landlord, won too from the rocks and the whins. He was the last of the line. The name would go to the grave with him.

Marion felt sure now that she was pregnant. The only remaining hope was the postal pregnancy test. She would slip quietly away after a couple of months. Tom never need know. She must love him all right. In spite of all she was going through she did not blame him. There was still a chance, the test. "With God's help..."

"I wonder were they talking about the Blessed Virgin behind her back, having a baby, and not married to Joseph?"

"I suppose they were," Tom answered. "It was nearly worse on Joseph, not knowing who the father was."

"The man wouldn't be blamed anyway," Marion said, a little venom in her voice. "I suppose his mates were clapping him on the back. 'Fair play to you, Joseph. You never lost it.'"

"Most of us think it was awful for Jesus to be born in a stable far from home but maybe they were just as pleased to get out of Nazareth at the time. Maybe that's why they didn't go back either until he was growing up a bit. People wouldn't know if they were married or not when he was born."

Mick Macken came to the door at about four in the morning. He looked wild and dishevelled. He started to say something to Tom, then stopped, shamefacedly. He took out a five-pound note. "Say a mass for my mother, Father," he said, and went away, half running in the night. Tom found it hard to understand what it was all about. "Christmas affects people in strange ways."

St Stephen's Day dawned on a blanket of white snow. The wren-boys were out early on the island. They wanted to have their job done early—there were to be currach races in the afternoon. It was the island's turn to have the races. Currachs had been coming from the mainland since early morning. The biggest difference between that day's races and the summer ones was that there was just one long race, between the best teams from each side. The day was too short for a plethora of smaller races.

The island team had been beaten in each of the previous three years. They were full of confidence this year, however. The team that had crossed to get the priest to anoint Bridgie was staying together for this occasion. Patcheen John and Jack Phaddy had refused to share the same currach for a number of years before that.

Although all three were over forty there was not a

shadow of doubt but that they were the best team on a stormy sea. It remained to be seen how they would fare on a frosty day without a whisper of wind. The team that had swept the boards for three years now represented the village, Mick Macken in front, and two of the Jenningses, who had represented Trinity, as oarsmen with him. The course was to take them around two currachs, anchored as markers a couple of miles from the shore, and end at the slip.

The currachs were prepared slowly and with great care for the race. Nothing would be left to chance. Oars and tholepins were tested. They were placed in line. Peadar Rua, who had been in the First World War, was given the honour of firing the shotgun. There was a great cheer when he raised the gun. He fired. The race was on.

The currachs leaped forward together. They stayed side by side, stroke for stroke of the oars, for a long time. Then the men on the island began slowly to inch in front. By the time they reached the first marker they were almost a currach length in front. The other currach's prow struck them broadside on as they turned. It did no damage to the boat but knocked them off their stroke and broke Patcheen's right-hand oar. If there had been any power in Jack Phaddy's curses, the mainland currach would have sunk in seconds. Instead of that, it pulled steadily away, gaining momentum all the time.

The hearts of the islanders sank as they looked out from the shore. It looked like four in a row for the village. "The calm doesn't suit our lads," said Peadar Rua. "It's a pity there isn't a bit of wind."

"That's the only way you'd win," the villagers

mocked, "if ye had a sail. But that's not allowed."

Coming to the second mark there were two lengths between the currachs but the islanders gained ground with an excellent turn. Now it was anybody's race. They were coming straight for the slip and it was not very easy to judge which was in front. The different rowing styles could be clearly seen, however, the islanders stroking deep and long, the villagers dipping the points of the oars quickly and often.

There was little between them. The shouting and cheering increased. "Keep it up, lads."

"Up *an baile s'againne*."

"Come on the village."

"*An t-oileán abú.*"

"Come on, lads," said Patcheen, leaning so far forward on his oars that his backside rose from the seat. His exertions produced a loud fart.

"That's it, lads," Jack Phaddy shouted. "Give it everything you have."

They were rowing in unison now as never before. They strained and stretched as one man. At the end they made the currach slide like a thoroughbred past the men of the village, winning by four lengths.

They were carried shoulder high to Collins's pub, pride and joy bursting the hearts of the islanders, not just because they had won the cup, but because of their heroics on behalf of old Bridgie Hughie.

"Three cheers for Patcheen's fart," shouted Jack Phaddy. "Let it never be said that we didn't have the wind behind us anyway."

Two barrels of Guinness had been set up in a corner of the island hall. Everyone on the island that could move was present as well as maybe a hundred people from the village who had stayed over after the races. St Stephen's night was the big night out of the year. Inhibitions were drowned in port and porter. The beat of the music, the swirl of the dance, the spirit and spirits of Christmas created an intense feeling of excitement and abandonment. In each break of the dance, ballads and *sean-nós* songs were sung.

Marion Warde had come over with the village girls, Eibhlín and Mary Phádraic Mhichilín who were home from the United States and their sister Barbara on holiday from secondary school in the city. Barbara had her eye on Paddy McEvilly. He had sat beside her on the bus on her way back to the convent after the previous Easter holiday. He was on his way to buy monofilament nets for illegal salmon fishing. She liked him, the hairy-faced island man with the reputation of being a communist, quiet, strong, surprisingly shy.

They had gone to a city pub together. She was barely sixteen but had drunk three vodkas. She had got sick in the chapel at night prayer. The nuns were full of sympathy, thinking she was seasick. Mainland and island was all the same to them, all back of the beyond.

Paddy was not taking much notice of her now. He stood with men of his own age who were home from England. None of them seemed interested in anything but their pints. Barbara had a couple of dances with Marion and with her sisters. There was no man on the floor yet. The night was young.

Marion was feeling better than she had been for a fortnight. It did her good to have girls near her own age for company. It was her first time on the island and people had made her very welcome. She was not used to the Irish of the people and she was not very good at the dances but she felt at home. There was no point in killing herself with worry until she had a definite word from the doctor.

She looked over at Tom. He sat talking to Doc Jennings, one of the men who had rowed for the village earlier in the day. Doc was famous as a rugby player, a ladies' man and a long-time medical student. Tom looked well, she thought.

Doc was telling him why he had not darkened the door of "church, chapel or meeting house" in over ten years, except when on holiday at home, to satisfy his parents, in case "they pulled the rug" on him.

"I have a strong belief myself in the freedom of the individual and in religious freedom," Tom Connor said. "As far as I'm concerned it's up to each person whether he goes to church or not."

"I know you're a good man, Connor. People around here are very fond of you. But I don't believe in God and all the mumbo-jumbo the Church goes on with. I don't see rhyme nor reason in it, and I haven't since I was seven years old and I went to my first communion."

He brought up all the old chestnuts, Galileo, the Inquisition, Pius XII and the Nazis, Doctor Noël Browne's "mother and child" scheme of the late forties, Church riches, poverty, abortion, contraception. Tom agreed with most of it. He could not contradict it. Scandal is scandal.

"I agree with most of what you've been saying, but do you expect me to leave the Church because you don't believe in it? From my point of view the only way to change things is from the inside."

"You haven't a hope in Hell, or maybe in this case, Heaven," Doc said sarcastically. "You haven't a hope of

changing the Church. Let it be and it will fall apart
naturally inside twenty years. It's the likes of you that
gives it a good name."

"The Church will be strong in Ireland for much
longer than that. Getting stronger, moving more to the
right it is day after day."

"Why stick up for it so. You of all people. It's well
known why your arse was kicked out here."

"I'm not sticking up for it any more than the next. I
find fault with it but I see its good points too. That's
why I'm in it, up to the pin of my collar in it."

"I know well you can't say anything against it."

"You're not listening to what I'm saying."

"I am listening. OK, so I've a drop in me, so have
you. I wouldn't be talking to you if we had not. Tell me
one thing. Why are you a priest?"

"For the money, of course."

"You haven't enough money to rattle on a stone."

"It's hard to say what brought me into it the first
day. Whatever I felt then would be different to what I
feel about it now—that was fifteen years ago. The main
underlying reason would be a love for Christ and a
desire to spread his teaching."

"I can see myself that Christ was a good man but
why did they have to go and make a bloody God out of
him?"

"Don't blame me for that, though that's what I
believe, and I wouldn't want to change it."

"But for someone like me that doesn't swallow the
God bit?"

"If I felt that Jesus was but a man, I think I would
still want to follow his teaching. I think it makes a lot
of sense, that it's a reasonable method of living for the

person who wants to have peace of mind. Forgiveness is really a lot more sensible than driving yourself around the bend with anger and the desire for revenge. There's a lot of sense too in the Church's attitude to marriage and the family."

"There is one thing that drives me around the fucking bend—an old bachelor of a Pope or a bishop, or a priest for that matter, trying to tell me about sex."

"I thought you were a bachelor yourself."

"If I am itself I don't tell anyone what to do with their sexual lives. When you have had the ride as often as I have, you can start lecturing to me about sex."

"I bow to the expert."

"No need to be shaggin' sarcastic. Do you know what I think, Connor? I think you're a fraud. I think every one of ye jumping jesuses is a fraud. You're riding along on the backs of the people."

"I don't need a lecture from the son of a gombeen. I could give examples of who's really on the backs of the people, a shop that is anything but hygienic, prices at the whim of the shopkeeper."

"Bejasus I'm getting your dander up at last. You don't have to tell me what people think of my old man's shop. But that's really a red herring. You're getting away from you, your double standards, finding fault with the Church and staying in it at the same time. You haven't the guts to stand up like the old-time priests and say out what the Church really stands for. They're stupid but they have the courage of their stupid convictions. They're not on a popularity kick like you are."

"If I was on a popularity kick, I'd still be in the diocesan college. I would be regularly licking the bishop's arse. There are those that do it and it pays. They are sent on courses. They are promoted. One of them will be a bishop yet and walk on me and the likes of me."

"OK, you're not the bishop's buddy. That doesn't worry you. But would you care if the people here did not like you, if they weren't eating out of your hand? That's the reason you don't want to change anything— improve things around here. You would have to stand on a few toes, and you wouldn't be the popular people's priest you are, the men buying you pints, the women thinking the sun, moon and stars shine from you."

"If I knew how to improve things I wouldn't give a damn what anyone said. But a person has to get to know the people first, gain their confidence. I feel I'm long enough here now. That's why I announced meetings for next week."

"Look around you here tonight. A great night, thank God," (this said with a smile) "if ever there was one. There is a night like this every year. That's not much of a life. The young people won't stay if they can't have the same services and pastimes as they have in the city."

"Is it gone too far?"

"There isn't much can be done until a place is gone too far. Even though I've been having a bit of a go at you there, I think you're the only one in a position to do something about it. There is still a bit of notice taken of the priest. You wouldn't be the first one to help get a place on its feet. Notice will be taken if you raise enough hell in the Dáil and places like that on behalf of your community."

"Look, Doc, is this all a pipe-dream? Even though

there's very little being done, I spend a lot more time writing letters to officials and filling forms for people than I spend on my knees. I've had meetings with the county council, department officials, politicians. Remember that meeting in your own pub during the summer. Promises, promises…"

"I was at that meeting. It was by chance—I was behind the bar that day. It opened my eyes. It gave me an interest in the place. I know I'm behind a bit in the study. I could be finished long ago but the crack was too good. It was not fair to the old ones, but money's no object—I didn't like that dig about making it on the backs of the people, by the way. Let it pass… Maybe you're right. The gombeen man is the cutest hoor in the country, and there has been a bit of that cuteness handed on in my genes. I'll be finished in a year and a half. When the internship and all that is over, I intend to come back here as GP, marry a virgin, of course, and live happily ever after. A nice dream, but will there be anything left except old people?"

"There will be more of them than there will be virgins—despite all my preaching."

"Did anything at all come of that meeting in the summer?"

"Not a single thing. Those officials were over the top anyway, promising everything that was asked for. If they could concentrate on one thing at a time."

"Something will have to be done."

"What about doing something yourself? What amazes me is the fine education so many young people from here have, and they never seem to think of putting anything back in their own place."

"Sure they're educated away from it and out of it.

Anyway who's going to take any notice—a prophet without honour, or whatever the man said? Who will listen to 'mac an tSeoinín' or anyone else for that matter? They might listen to you."

"If I could get a crowd up to the Dáil, would you be able to organise things at that end?"

"I'll look after the bed and breakfast—it might be rough. I'll see to publicity. What is there to lose? I'm sure you can see from the baptismal register how the population is going."

"It doesn't take a book to tell me. I can count them on one finger."

There was a laugh when two of the girls, swirling too quickly as they danced the "Stack of Barley" tripped each other up and ended in a heap on the floor. The dance was getting lively.

"By the way," said Jack. "What's that one that's staying with you like?"

"It's up to you to find that out."

"I'm going to do just that."

Barbara Phádraic Mhichilín felt it was time to attract Paddy McEvilly's attention. She liberally sprayed herself with her sister's perfume when they visited the bathroom. She checked her hair in the mirror, ruffled it a bit, straightened her dress.

Some of her own family thought Barbara a bit spoiled, that she had sought too much attention because her sister, Teresa, was handicapped, and therefore herself the centre of attention. While Barbara loved Teresa, she found boarding-school a great freedom, since she had spent her youth minding her sister.

She was the brightest girl in the class, something

that overcame the snobbery shown by paying students towards those subsidised by the state. She envied the city girls the social life they were always talking about. She longed to have her Leaving Cert so that she could spread her wings, with a flat of her own, discos, dances, boyfriends. She always asked the most difficult questions in religion class to show the city slickers that she knew more about everything from sex to theology than any of them.

Apart from a few kisses and a bit of groping behind the hall in holiday times, she had had little to do with boys. It would be different with Paddy McEvilly. She knew that she was in love with him.

The man she felt she loved had his eye on another. He had a fancy for Marion Warde, whom he had met once or twice when he called in to see the priest on the mainland. She was out dancing with Doc Jennings, so he felt he did not have much of a chance there.

"Howya?" Barbara was standing beside him.

"Hello." He felt suddenly shy and awkward.

"I didn't see you in the city since."

"You have a good memory. I stay out of there as much as I can."

"How did the fishing go? You were going to buy a net the last time I met you." She felt she had to keep talking. He might walk away if she had nothing to say. He felt much the same.

"We did well at the start. We had twenty one day. Then the bloody bailiff took the net."

The "Siege of Ennis" started. Barbara caught his hand and whisked him out on the floor, to make up a foursome with her sister and Jackie Reilly.

"Bygones be bygones?" Jackie proffered a hand.

Paddy was reluctant. "What the hell," he thought. Old enmities seemed trivial when there were girls about. Girls made all the difference. He shook hands, a rueful smile on his face.

"You would want to be fit out there." Barbara, a little overweight, was red in the face with the exertion of the dance. She sat on his knee. "I'm dying with the thirst."

"Have a drop of this." He held out his mug of porter.

"Great stuff. Can you get me a full one?"

"What would Pádraic Mhichilín say if he saw me giving porter to his little daughter."

"I'm not little, and anyway it's doctor's orders. My blood is weak or something." Paddy signalled to Johnny Collins to send down two more mugs.

There was a great cheer from the crowd when Peadar Rua took to the floor on his own to dance a reel. Marcas Phaddy soon joined him. Then Shamey Fitz, almost sixty years younger than them. Shamey still carried his drink, each jump sending porter spray in the air. Big Mick Macken went out too, banging his hobnailed heels in perfect time to the music. He had not danced for twenty years but what was in the head was in the feet as well. He felt great.

For a while now he had felt a weight of depression and loneliness. He didn't understand it or know where it came from. Christmas was always lonely for a person on his own but this had started long before Christmas.

It was often said that Mick Macken could have had the pick of the parish but that no girl was good enough for him. That was not the reason he had not married. He had never thought he wouldn't marry. Life just seemed to have passed him by. The young women had all gone away, married in England and America. Maybe he should have gone too but he had the bit of land and his mother had lived until a few years before. He was settled and comfortable. Why should he have gone away?

He had been thinking for a while now of suicide. Trying to get it out of his mind he had gone to the priest on Christmas night, after a heavy drinking session. He didn't know what he wanted, company, a cure of some kind. His nerve had failed. He couldn't say what he wanted to say. All that was now forgotten in the drink and the dance.

It was late. Children were brought home. The women went around with tea and sandwiches. The party would last until dawn, when the currachs would have daylight for their journey home. The younger people began to slip away. It was far better to be off than listening to speeches as the cup was presented.

Jack Phaddy in his acceptance speech for the cup quoted a sentence made famous by the recipient of some long-forgotten honour: "I want to thank you from the bottom of my heart, and from my wife's bottom as well."

Barbara Phádraic Mhichilín was happy. She lay with Paddy McEvilly in her arms. It was her first time. It had not hurt her at all. The nuns were wrong about that too. They would tell you anything to keep you from doing it.

Paddy was ashamed of himself. He had pulled out too quickly and squirted all over Barbara's belly. "Sorry," he said. "I'm sorry."

"I love you," Barbara said.

He was ashamed, ashamed that he had not lasted longer, ashamed at having done it at all. She was so young, and they had done nothing to prevent conception. Barbara was kissing him, big wet warm kisses. "Paddy, I love you. I have loved you since that day we were together in the bus."

He wondered where she had learned to talk like that, had she done it often, or learned it from women's magazines? He lay on his back. Barbara had her head on his shoulder, her leg, in a long leather boot, thrown across him. She ran her fingers through the hair on his chest.

"Are you tired?"

"No."

"You're very quiet."

"I suppose I'm a bit ashamed and worried."

"Why?"

Paddy did not reply. She stroked his nose with her finger.

"Don't let that worry you."

"Why?"

"No why."

"It could happen."

"It won't."

"You're very sure."

"I'm on the pill."

"You do this often?"

"You should know that."

"What should I know?"

"I was never with anyone, like that, before."

"Why the pill so?"

"The doctor put me on it. I wasn't having...well...

periods right. I wasn't regular. My blood is weak, or something."

"Whatever is weak, it certainly isn't your heart." He felt her heartbeat, caressed her breasts. Their bodies were soon woven together again. Once there was no danger of pregnancy all inhibitions, all conscientious objections, faded. They fell asleep in each other's arms.

They had left the hall before the speeches, and walked hand in hand down to the beach. The sea reflected the almost full moon. They threw stones in the tide. Barbara splashed Paddy. He chased, caught her easily when her high heels sank in the sand. He carried her down to the water, pretending he was going to throw her in.

"You can't refuse a last request," she said.

"OK, but be quick about it."

"A kiss, from the handsomest man on the island."

"It might not be easy to find him, this time of night."

"I do not have to go very far." You would really think it was her last kiss—it went on for so long, tongues searching, intertwining. When they stopped to draw breath the tide was coming up on their shoes. Paddy took off his shoes, squeezed his socks. Barbara tried to stand on his toes.

"Stop."

"It will keep them warm."

"Your own toes will be frozen in a minute in those wellingtons."

"Yourself and your wellingtons. These are patent leather boots. Anyway they say sea water never did anyone any harm."

"It drowned enough of people."

"You're so smart. A wetting from salt water…"

"It might not have done harm to someone walking or working. It's different standing around on a frosty night."

"Come on so. Run and it will warm us up."

They ran, arms around each other, falling with laughter, Barbara's fashionable boots most unsuitable for walking or running on an island road in the middle of the night.

"I know what we'll do," Paddy said. "I'll light a fire, to warm us up, or you'll be dying with the frostbite before the currachs go across in the morning."

"What will your mother say if you arrive home with a girl you have nearly drowned?"

"I don't mind what she would say. I'm twenty-one. But it's not the house I'm talking about. There's a little hut back here under the drop of the crag. There's a gas ring in it—I make a turn of poteen now and again. I'll make a drop of punch to heat us up."

"Any excuse for a drink."

Inside the hut that his grandfather had built at the turn of the century there was a poteen still hidden in the hay. Paddy lit the gas-ring, large enough to boil a barrel of water. He put a saucepan of neat poteen on it, adding sugar for fermenting purposes from the catering pack he had with him. The poteen with the water evaporated was extremely strong. They sat together on the hay, drinking from the only mug.

"I thought you were going to show me the worm."

Paddy smiled.

"The worm for making the poteen, you dirty ould devil."

"I didn't say anything."

"I know well what you were thinking."

"They say the dirt is in the mind of the one that sees it."

He rooted in the hay for the worm. She hid his socks while he was not looking. Eventually he pulled out the copper spiral.

"Isn't it awful twisted, whatever it's for."

"Who has the dirty mind now?"

"You have lovely toes," Barbara said, tickling him with a blade of straw.

"What did you do with my socks?" Paddy said, leaping around on one foot.

"Maybe they were burned in the fire. I could smell something awful a while ago." Paddy caught her and they wrestled in the hay. Soon they were kissing. When Barbara whispered, "Make love to me," they had gone too far to stop.

It was after six when they awoke, nearly time for Barbara to go home. Paddy promised to visit her often in the city. It would make life in the convent a lot easier.

It was very cold on the sea at that time of the morning. The only ones able to keep warm were the men rowing. Lying asleep in the prow of Mick Macken's currach was Seán Mhichil, a boy of about fifteen, his face the colour of death. He had left the dance early and it was clear that he was almost unconscious with alcohol when he was carried down to the currach. By the time he was brought ashore he was stiff. It was impossible to waken him. He was carried home on a litter, made by tying a few oars together.

After some severe questioning his companions

admitted that he had drunk porter, wine and poteen. When they failed to waken him from a drunken stupor they had dipped his head in the tide. The shock of the cold water awakened him for a few moments but he soon lapsed into a drunken sleep again.

The telephone lines were out. The only people around with medical training were Doc Jennings and the nurse. Doc slapped him on the face and soles of the feet to see if he would react or respond. He agreed with the nurse that an injection would be dangerous. It might put him in a coma. His mother prayed. She also cursed the people who had given an "innocent little boy" intoxicating drink. She pleaded with the priest to bring back her son, "as the Lord did for the widow of Naim." She was a widow too. Everybody was full of sympathy for her but few would agree with her assessment of her son as one of the holy innocents.

"Seán, Seáinín," Doc shouted and slapped.

"Waken up, Seáinín, a mhac."

"Fuck off!" Seáinín pushed Doc's hand away.

"Where did he learn to talk like that, Father?" All Tom Connor cared was that he was alive, and recovering. "Those were the sweetest words I heard in a long time, ma'am."

There was a big meeting on the island on New Year's Day. Those home on holiday joined the rest of the population in the hall. Tom Connor started the meeting like an opposition politician beginning an election campaign. He made a list of the promises that had been made by government departments since he had come to live and work among them.

"It is seven months now since we were promised a

proper pier and landing facilities. We were told the money was there, the plans drawn up. Has there been anything heard of it since?

"At the same meeting we were promised a proper ferry service, a mailboat suitable for the conditions on the ocean we have to put up with. Did anything happen since?

"We were promised a survey to see if the sandhills were suitable for a grass airstrip. Have we heard or seen anyone since?

"When the telephone link is broken, as it often is, we could all be dead and buried unknown to the world. Who is going to do anything about fulfilling the promise of a proper telephone service?

"What about the basic facilities people all over the world call civil rights? Electricity and a water supply are some of the most basic of those. What about work, for girls especially, so that the island may have some future?

"Do we care? Have things gone so far that we cannot do anything? In other words, is this place already finished? Are we, are you, the last generation?"

He didn't attempt any answers. He stood on the stage, looking down at the table in front of him, waiting for what he had said to sink in. There was nothing new in what he said, nothing that was not well known already. Compared to other meetings people seemed very quiet, ready to listen intently. They had been patient long enough.

Tom Connor began again in a low voice but high enough to be heard in the silent hall. "It is high time to tell this government to give up using this place on advertisements and pictures to attract tourists. Let them give us the same standard of living as people have on the mainland, or change us out altogether. How much would that cost them?

"Unless all the fine talk about culture and the Irish language is complete hypocrisy, we have something precious here. Is it unreasonable for us to ask for a decent standard of living? If something is not done soon there will be no culture, no language, no people left. There will be nothing but the seagulls."

The applause was quiet, respectful, when he sat down. They had heard it all before. Why should this time be different?

Marcas Phaddy had never opened his mouth at a public meeting before. He stood up. He told of the bill for £2.11 and the threat to sell his land from under his feet, as he put it himself.

"I am an old man—until now a patient old man. I have voted for the party in government since it was founded. I have seen a lot in my time, here and in England, but nothing ever upset me as much as that letter. I agree with the priest. It's time for us to put up a fight to win fair play for ourselves."

Referring to Marcas's letter Tom Connor told of how he had written to the papers complaining about the treatment meted out to Marcas and to people like him. None of them had published it. The Irish language radio seemed too close to the politicians to ask any serious questions on behalf of the people. They were on their own. They should go to the gates of Dáil Éireann and tell the politicians and the whole country how badly they were being treated.

People were getting more vocal as the meeting warmed up. Some of the young people said they would stay at home if there was work available. If there was work, there would be people. If there were people there would be a good social life.

Paddy McEvilly stayed quiet but he was delighted. He felt he would put some of the people off if he made radical proposals so he kept his mouth shut. He felt that all his advice and encouragement to the young people to speak out was not wasted after all.

Jack Phaddy formally proposed a picket on Dáil Éireann as soon as the TDs got back after their Christmas recess—"even if it takes them until Easter to do so." They would not leave until the Minister for the Gaeltacht and other relevant ministers met them. They would then give them three months to show they were serious about whatever they would promise. If nothing had happened by then they would go on hungerstrike.

The meeting was five minutes settling down after Jack's speech, people shouting and cheering. The schoolmistress seconded Jack's proposal as soon as there was enough calm. It was carried unanimously. The time had come for action.

A church-gate collection was arranged for the following Sunday to defray expenses incurred by travelling to Dublin. Everyone that could travel would do so, with Jack Phaddy, the priest and Paddy McEvilly as spokesmen. It came as a big surprise to Paddy to find Jackie Reilly propose him. "Bygones must really be going to be bygones," he thought.

The meeting on the mainland was much different. It was held in Tigh Sheoinín, as there was no community hall there—the island hall had been subsidised by the Gaeltacht Department. Doc Jennings opened the meeting, proposing immediately that they follow the good example of the people of the island and join them in the picket on Dáil Éireann. Tom Connor seconded the motion. It was a bad tactical move, as the villagers felt themselves a step above the islanders.

"We are not nearly as badly off as they are, out there on the high seas," Jack Jennings, Doc's father, said. "We are not nearly as backward. We have the road to our doorsteps, and if we are patient and follow the proper channels we will gain all the advantages the young people are rightly seeking." His voice rose. "I myself will speak to the Taoiseach, who I am proud to number among my personal friends. I have no doubt that he will give me a sympathetic hearing."

He continued by saying that he agreed that the government process was a slow one. "Don't forget that they have problems too, the national debt, crime, and, most important of all, the regaining of all the land of the nation." Their own problems seemed great but they were small when viewed from the national stand-point. It would be a great mistake to have the government think that they were not grateful. There was not a house in the parish that had not an income because of the generosity of the government party. They might seem badly off when compared with what could be seen in the pictures but they were better off than the people of the cities who had neither land nor shore.

"I think my own son here and Father Connor deserve great praise in organising this meeting but I cannot say that I agree with this picketing. There are more civilised ways of doing things."

Tom Connor was livid. He knew their cause was lost when the great man himself did not throw in his lot with them. Patronising bastard! There was nothing to lose now, so he asked a question. "When you say, Mr Jennings, that the people of the island are backward, is it the Irish language you are referring to?" He knew that it was not a fair question but he was angry at the prospect of the old man getting his way again.

"You know as well as I do, Father, that I would not say such a thing about people who make up, whether I like it or not, half my customers. It is not the language that makes the island backward but the sea. As an intelligent and educated man, Father, you know that the revival of the Irish language is one of the major aims of the party to which I belong and to which I have belonged from the beginning." His voice took on an emotional timbre.

"Long before you were born, men of my generation went out to fight so that we could have our own country and language and culture. And it was not placards we had on our shoulders."

The old grey head shook with anger—anger that anyone should question his political credentials, and above all a priest. He had always befriended the priests. Down through the years there was not one of them that had not played cards in his house on Sunday nights. How often had he brought them to the city for a game of golf or to a play or some such civilised pursuit. That helped keep them sane when they had no one to talk to on their level.

There was a different kind of priest being produced in the latter years. The new ones thought that poker, bridge and golf were big-shot games. They tried to be like the ordinary people, drinking pints in pubs and dancing at weddings. They lost the respect of the quality people in this way. It showed how low the standards of the priesthood had fallen due to the shortage of vocations. The day seemed to have come that the Church accepted anyone who would give the priesthood a try. This led to a preponderance of children from tradesman and labourer backgrounds being ordained. The standard of civility and culture had slipped.

Old Jack still had the power earned by his father and mother through years of honest trade. He was a man in the old mould, a staunch Catholic who spared no expense in sending his children to the best, or at least the most expensive, schools. He was proud that he was able to deliver ninety per cent of the vote to his party, a small enough return, really, he felt, for years of generous credit in the hard times. He was the anchor of the community, more conservative than the priests, a continuum while they came and went.

Jack Jennings was delighted that his son was at last beginning to show, not just interest, but leadership potential. He was still a bit wild but youth would be forgiven its extravagances. Rural Ireland had always been tolerant of the wild oats of the better class of people, the children of schoolteachers, doctors and shopkeepers, when they were at university. Although he did not personally agree with the picket "Doc", as everyone called him, proposed, it would stand to him in the long run that he had spoken out on behalf of the poorer people. It would stand to him when the day long anticipated by his father came, the day he would get a nomination to stand for one of the safest parliamentary seats in Ireland.

No one spoke after Jack Jennings. The meeting ended with nothing arranged except that Jack would have a word in the ear of his old friend, the Taoiseach.

Forty islanders travelled by coach to Dublin. They rowed across from the island at six o'clock in the morning in six currachs. Tom Connor joined them in the bus. They had breakfast in Galway and reached Dublin about midday. There was persistent heavy rain. It was ironical that people who spent much of their lives in oilskins had left them at home. Wearing their Sunday clothes they were drenched a half-hour after arriving at the gates of the Dáil.

A garda at the gate told them the TDs would not be there until about three o'clock. When they found that the minister for the Gaeltacht was in Kerry for an official opening, spirits sank. They began to complain about the rain and the lack of organisation. Patcheen John proposed that they go to a public house or hotel until the TDs came back.

"What would people think of a crowd of drunks at the gates of the Dáil?" Jack Phaddy asked.

"You would think that a drink never crossed your lips the way you are talking. What's the point of being here when there are no TDs. It's like a pub with no beer, a Dáil with no TDs."

"I don't know what brought you here if you cannot put up with a dropeen of rain."

"You're one of the organisers. Wouldn't we be a lot better at home searching for wrack, than to be standing here like *amadáns*."

"Maybe you look like an *amadán*..."

Two taxis pulled up beside them. Immediately they were surrounded by reporters, Doc Jennings directing operations. "There will be more cameras here in a little while, and a current affairs programme wants to speak to representatives," Doc said.

"Will it not look strange to be picketing a parliament without members?"

"It doesn't matter a damn so long as this hits the evening news-stands. In fact we're better off without them at the moment. They would have some mealy-mouthed answer for the cameras. If the news headlines carry this on the hour you'll have ministers and TDs licking your arses before the evening is out."

Doc's assessment was correct. The evening papers had headlines like "Homespun protest," and "'We've had enough,' says rebel priest."

About half past three some of the local TDs came out to meet them. The two from the government party said they already had arranged for a delegation to meet a senior minister. The opposition advised them not to meet anyone but stay on the streets in order to gain maximum publicity and shame the government.

They did a little of both—sent spokesmen to meet the minister while the others remained picketing on the street outside.

"This is not normal practice," the minister said when four glasses of brandy were brought in on a tray, "but you must be drowned wet standing out there in the rain."

"Don't get the impression that we can be bought off with brandy," Paddy McEvilly said, having finished his glass in one gulp. "You're showing an interest in us now that we have got a bit of publicity. We would not be here at all if a bit of interest was paid us at any time other than during election campaigns. Even then it's little interest that's shown because you have most of the vote sewn up. The place that's at the bottom of your list of priorities is left there—at the bottom of the barrel."

The minister was a big man, slightly overweight, curly black hair combed back from his forehead, a mixture of troubleshooter and pourer of oil on troubled waters for the government.

"Listen, young man,"—he looked Paddy straight in the eye—"this government does not accept delegations at short notice from every element of the lunatic fringe that stands outside the gates of Dáil Éireann. I am not here to listen to *seafóid*. If you have problems to solve tell me about them and I will make an effort to help you. Now, Father,"—he turned to Tom Connor—"what's your problem?"

"No problem, personally, that is." His attempt at a joke did not wear well with a minister famous not only for his positive attitude, but also for the phrase, "No problem."

"I would prefer if Paddy here, or Jack, were to tell you the problems of the island. I'm only there a couple of years. They have spent their lives there and want to continue to do so—if the proper services and facilities are made available."

"I do not mind who speaks but I'm not going to sit listening to recriminations and tales of past woes. We are talking about what needs to be and what can be done. Now Paddy…"

"Your island certainly has problems," the minister said when Paddy was finished. "Most of them can be solved with goodwill and money. I will immediately contact my fellow-members of the cabinet, and the Taoiseach, of course. I guarantee that you will see things begin to happen inside a few weeks."

"If they don't begin to happen you'll be seeing us sooner than you expect," said Jack Phaddy. "We'll be here occupying your office and on hunger-strike as well."

"I am a man of my word who does not appreciate threats. If I am to help it is not to keep you out of my office or away from my gate. I will help because you have big problems, you have made a good case and deserve the same rights as everyone else. I personally guarantee that your visit to Dublin has not been in vain. Now who would drink another brandy?"

They called off the picket when they went out to the rest of the group and told their story. TDs from their own constituency arranged a meal for them in the Shelbourne hotel, as well as rooms to dry their clothes. Some went to visit relatives. All came together at ten o'clock in the *Conradh na Gaeilge* club, where they had a night to remember. It was very late when the bus left Merrion Street.

Marion listened to Tom speaking on the radio as she got ready to leave. The pregnancy test was positive. She felt she had no choice except to go. She would slip away quietly before he returned from Dublin. The radio news mentioned that he and other members of the delegation would be on a current affairs television programme the following night. She would be on a bus before that, and away.

What surprised her most was that she seemed to feel nothing. She had expected to be all emotional, resenting the child, hating Tom, cursing God. She felt nothing except the desire to go through the motions of packing her clothes, get through the night and be on the bus in the morning.

She would go to London again. She would prefer not to have to, but she knew her way around, and there was anonymity there. There were organisations too that would help if she needed them.

It was strange that the last time she would hear Tom's voice was this disembodied sound from the small black box of a radio. He talked with conviction of the problems of island living: isolation, danger on the sea, lack of work, emigration, the language that was being let die with the people. He spoke of the way small problems can become big ones on an island, molehills mountains.

For a moment Marion had a pang of great sadness, a desire to record his voice, have something to remember him by, maybe someday play the recording to their child. She felt then she would have to get a grip on herself, forget, force closed the sluice-gates of memory, survive without him, survive, survive.

What would she write on the note? Something that would ease his mind, make him think the old wander-lust had struck again? Or the truth?

She made herself a hot punch. Strong. She left the bottle beside the bed. She might need it if she could not sleep. She set the clock for nine. She would get the bus at ten. That would be the worst part, leaving the place she had been happiest. Better not think of it. Away, away.

"Those fucking French letters," she heard herself say, and found that she was laughing, forgetting her troubles for a moment, remembering a story Tom had told her of Irish Catholic girls in a condom factory in

England. They salved their consciences by sticking a pin in each condom, to leave them "open to life," the theological distinction that was the lynchpin of their Church's argument for the difference between "natural" and "unnatural" forms of love-making. Laughter turned as quickly to tears. They would never share a joke again. Maybe they had shared too much.

Marion cried hot and bitter tears in her loneliness and desolation. Whiskey is a poor companion when you are in a big empty room on your own. She cried out in her agony, mostly in heartbreak, partly hoping to cry herself out, as it were, so that she would be composed as she went on the bus in the morning. She had no control now of the sobs that racked her body. She never remembered such misery.

She drifted into sleep at last, a heavy drugged sleep. It was Tom's cold feet that awakened her, as he slipped into bed.

"Who...Who's that?"

"Mick Macken." She laughed and put her arms around him. "What time is it?"

"A quarter past seven. The bus is just back. God help the rest of them, they have to row across to the island yet."

She then remembered the day just gone, realised that she had not been dreaming. "I thought you were not to get back until tomorrow."

"Why? Did you not know that I couldn't go another day without you?" He hugged her.

"It said on the radio that you were to be on television tonight."

"That's true, but it was recorded yesterday—or was it today? You get mixed up in the days when you're up all night."

"Ye got on well according to the radio?"

"Great, if the minister keeps his word. We'll have to just wait and see, but no way will we let him go back on his promises."

Tom recounted everything that happened, almost word for word, everything clear as a bell in his mind, as things often are when someone has out-of-the-ordinary experiences. "And how are you yourself since?"

"Nothing new here. A couple of people called with mass cards or something. They had forgotten that you were going up with the islanders. They will call again."

"I hope that they don't come back too soon. I could sleep for a week."

"You won't be disturbed."

"Are you thinking of going to town? I saw bags."

"When I thought you would be away..."

"It looks like a lot of bags for a day in town."

Marion was silent.

"You're not thinking of going or anything." Tom straightened up in the bed and put on the light, alarmed. "I know I've been away a lot, but with the meetings, and the protest. I'll have more time..."

Marion was crying.

"Marion. What's wrong, what have I done?" He tried to put his arms around her but she pushed him away. "Were you frightened on your own? I'd have brought back a present if we had a chance to go to the shops."

She did not answer. He did not know what to do. "I'll never understand women. I thought you'd be pleased for me... Is this pre-menstrual tension or what?"

"I wish to fuck it was—you're so stupid."

"You're not pregnant?"

Marion buried her head in the pillow and sobbed. Tom felt shattered. He had been on such a high. The papers had made a little god of him, the Moses who was going to lead his island into the promised land. He had begun to believe the publicity. And now this.

"And you were going away before I came back?" Marion looked him in the face. "It's not going to do you any harm. No one will know, except God, if there is one. There couldn't be." She burst out crying again, turned from him when he tried to put his arms about her.

"When did you find out?"

Marion answered quietly. "I found out for definite yesterday. I've had a good idea for a fortnight or more."

"Why didn't you tell me?"

"There was a chance until yesterday that it was only a false alarm."

"Is it mine?" He knew it was a mean lousy question, anything to get himself off the hook.

"What kind of fucking bastard are you?" Marion tried to hit him but he held her arms.

"I'm sorry...I know, I know you weren't with any-one else. But it has come as such a shock. We always took precautions."

"Well, one of your rotten precautions must have burst. I thought I knew you. How could you think I would be with anyone, and me married to you in all but name. As if there was any man in the place. I'm glad now I didn't go before you came back. I know now what kind of a man you are. Just like the rest of them— have your fun and run."

"You're the one that's running."

"Don't let that worry you. I will be on the bus in a couple of hours, out of your way, out of your life. If the radio and the papers knew that yesterday's hero isn't such a hero after all."

"Marion. Please, please forgive what I said. Think of the shock I've just had. You have been thinking of it for two weeks or more. It didn't cross my mind until now. I haven't slept for two days. I don't know what's happening."

"You'll be able to tell your priest friends that you have proved your manhood, even though you're not acting like a man."

"Don't be like that, Marion. I'm sorry that stupid question slipped out on me."

Marion lit a cigarette and sat against the pillows. Neither spoke for a long time. It was Tom who broke the silence.

"Even if you want to go, you do not have to go today."

"It is for the best, for both of us."

"Can you not give me time to think, to try and work something out?"

"Everything is worked out. I'm going, that is that."

"There are other choices, plenty of them."

"What are they?"

"I could go with you. We can marry, you could stay and have the child here." He was racking his brains for some way to prevent her going on that morning's bus.

"And what about the obvious choice?"

"What?"

"Don't pretend you're so fucking innocent—abortion. I suppose you never heard talk of it."

"I don't agree with it."

"Why didn't you think of that before now?"

"Don't be like that, Marion. I'm trying to be reasonable."

"Be reasonable so."

"I cannot stop you if you want to have an abortion, but I don't want you to. I'll leave, anything."

"I don't want to either. I have thought of every possibility for a fortnight. The only way is for me to go."

"You may be right, I don't know. But why have you to go today? It won't be born tomorrow."

"Your prayers might be answered. I might miscarry. Then we could carry, or miscarry, on as we were."

"Please don't be so sarcastic. I love you. I didn't want, didn't expect this to happen. A couple of days, a couple of weeks aren't going to make any difference. It will just give us enough time to think clearly."

"It would be harder to go then than now."

"It will be hard whatever we decide. I know and I appreciate why you wanted to go today—to save my bacon. I'm grateful. But I'm home now. I know about it. That changes the whole complexion of it."

"Maybe it does. O, Tom, I'm so mixed up. I don't want to go away and us fighting, but I don't see any other way."

"All I'm asking is that you do not go today."

"I want to remember us as we were—in love." Her eyes filled with tears. He burst out crying too, and they lay in each other's arms together.

"I'm sorry for the things I said," Marion whispered through her tears. "I will never hate you or our child. I will give him as much love as both of us could. But you will have to let me go. I don't want to see you crucified by the bishop or the people, and I don't think you should leave the priesthood—you would not be satisfied in any other walk of life."

"I will not be satisfied in the priesthood either if I go against my conscience, if I do not accept responsibility for my own actions the very thing I would expect from anyone in the parish."

"We'll work something out."

"You won't go today, so?"

"Maybe it would be better."

"It would not."

"We'll see. You must be starving with the hunger. I'll get something to eat."

Tom lay on the bed, overtired, full of nerves, unable to sleep. How could he sleep when his world had just crashed down about his head? Why had he not thought of all that before they began to sleep together? He thought ruefully that the answer was probably in the old Latin tag: *Penis erectus non conscientiam habet.*

Neither spoke during the breakfast. The bus had come and would not be back for another two days.

"You should go to bed," Marion said at last, "You look killed tired."

"I couldn't sleep now. I think I will go for a walk. The sea air might blow the cobwebs off my brain."

"It's pouring rain."

"It doesn't matter. I'll cover myself well."

He put on his full oilskin suit and wellington boots. He kissed Marion's cheek before he left the house. "I'm so glad that you did not leave on that bus today."

"There will be another day. Say one for me, if it's going out to pray you are."

He is more of a pity than I am, Marion thought as

Tom trudged away in the rain. She would have the baby to remember their love by. All he would have was his sterile Church. In any other denomination the news that the wife of the clergyman was expecting their baby would bring joy to the community of faith. But in the Roman Catholic Church...

Tom headed for the cliffs, a place he often went to sort out his thoughts, say a prayer, work out a sermon, or to get peace of mind from just looking at the great waves break in on the shore. It was a rough walk to the clifftop but not at all steep as the land rose slowly. The ground was paved with jagged and broken pieces of limestone, serried rows of rock, as if a sea had suddenly frozen.

Looking down from the top of the cliff, he knew that suicide was one of the options that faced him now, an easy escape from his problems. He did not know if he had the courage. The killing part would be quick and easy. What about the other side?

He sat for a while counting the waves, trying to forget his troubles, so that he could see things clearer when he came back to them. He had not been on the cliff since the night they had searched for Teresa Phádraic Mhichilín. He found it hard to understand how she had come safely through that place on a pitch-black night, her old dead sheepdog in her arms. He saw himself as carrying just as heavy a cross in just as dangerous a place.

Looking out to sea, the twin hills of the island looked like two old women huddled in conversation. They'll soon have plenty to talk about, he thought.

The easy option for him would be to let Marion go as she had planned. No one would be the wiser, but he would have to live with his conscience for the rest of his life. He would be turning his back on his own child. That was a stronger tie than the vow he made never to marry.

He thought back to that day in Maynooth, the day they made the vow of celibacy, the day of their subdiaconate, an order the Pope had dropped from the Church's ministry a few years later, but that celibacy was attached to at the time. They were in "Mary's" oratory. Stan Cunnance had brought in an effects pistol from the Aula Maxima. He sat in the back seat, the gun in his hand. "Ye'll have it to say," he said, "that ye took this vow with a gun at your backs."

Vow-taking was such a serious business that the safety valve of humour was necessary in order to preserve sanity. Celibacy tended to be equated with castration. There was one story of a line of students filing into the college chapel past a severe-looking archbishop who was decked out in ecclesiastical finery right down to the cloth-of-gold gloves. The significance of the gloves was not lost on one of the more Gaelic football-oriented students. "He must be expecting a wet ball today," was the immortal comment.

A pity that it was not castration, Tom thought to himself, I would not be in the trouble I'm in now. It was a wonder the Church had not gone that far, he thought, but they were satisfied if your balls were hung up by your own free will. They were not too satisfied with one of the fathers of the Church who was so zealous that he castrated himself. Poor Origen. They never made a saint out of him. But then he lived at a time celibacy was optional to the clergy, and they had more sense than to canonise castration.

Sitting on a rock in the rain, looking out to sea, he wondered what was the best option for himself and Marion to choose. They could leave and marry. How often had Marion said she did not want him to leave the priesthood? Still, this might change her mind.

What if she left and they stayed in touch rearing the child together, as other priests and other women had done?

Should they stay where they were, have the baby, brazen it out until the bishop or the parishioners, or both, gave them the road? He thought Marion would prefer to go than put herself through the likes of that. It would fit in with his own ideas of challenging celibacy. People living on the periphery of the world were unlikely to have earth-shattering effects on the Church, but if they had to leave was there anything to lose in making an issue of celibacy?

This would also gel with the idea of accepting responsibility for your actions. Which was morally more acceptable, to let Marion leave and rear their child on her own, or stay together and accept their responsibilities? The cross would be harder to carry but it would be shared. And if they had to go, they would.

He would be more interested in what his own congregation thought than in what the bishop thought. They would have a real chance if the people of the place stood up for them but there was more than that to be considered. There was the question of public morality. If the man preaching the word of God was living "in sin" would he be listened to when he encouraged people to live by the law of Christ and the commandments of God and the Church?

He was aware even as he considered that question

that people would not reject Christ because of the weakness of one of his ministers. If things were like that the Church would long since have fallen apart. Were not the apostles Christ chose weak? How many popes had led scandalous lives? He had often heard people say of the clergy, "Do what they say, not what they do." He understood it better than ever now.

He did not feel that Marion and he lived in sin. They were married in everything but name. If anything it was the law of the Church that prevented them marrying. Why, why did the man who wanted to be a priest have to forgo the love of a wife and a family? Somewhere, sometime, somehow the half-million or so priests in the world would have to take a stand on the question of compulsory celibacy, a stand other than opting out, as thousands had done in recent years. Tom had often heard from missionary priests that in faraway countries many of the priests had women and children. But they were far from Rome, and the Church could ill afford to do without them.

There was a chance that some people would accept it if Marion stayed and had the baby. Jack Phaddy and Mary surely, Paddy McEvilly because he would support anything revolutionary. Most of the younger people could hardly care. What about the older people, people like Marcas Phaddy, Peadar Rua, Mary Guiney, Pádraic Mhichilín? It would put their faith and friendship to a real test. And what about the defender of the conscience of the congregation himself—Tom Jennings, friend of bishops and taoisigh. He would drown them like a couple of kittens.

"Will you stay with me and fight it out until the end?" he asked Marion when he returned to the house.

"Go to your bed," she said, "before you lose the head altogether."

The result of the picket in Dublin was evident before very long. Six men arrived on the following Tuesday asking to hire currachs in the village to take them across to the island. Among them were officers from the Department of the Gaeltacht, the Gaeltacht Authority, the county council and the Office of Public Works.

The sea was choppy. Most of the officials were both sick and drenched to the skin in the currachs. Tom Connor, travelling with them, had no pity for them. It would show them how the islanders lived, make them appreciate their problems more.

They went first to see the sandhills to the north of the island. They pronounced the area suitable for airstrip development—similar schemes had worked well on the islands of Aran in Galway Bay. Bulldozers would have little trouble levelling the sandhills. A careful setting of marram grass would prevent the sand from blowing and the area being eroded.

Two surveyors were left there to measure the area, while the rest of the officials went to the hall for a meeting. There the county council engineer explained that they had quite a bit of money on hand. This had been granted in recent years for island roads but had not been spent because the islanders could not agree on who should get work on the schemes. "Vandals" had held up the work at every attempt that had been made to start a scheme. Walls were built across roads at night, shovels and other equipment stolen.

"You know well what caused the trouble," Paddy

McEvilly said, "but you're not satisfied to do anything about it. You put people to work straight from labour exchange lists. These are the people with decent dole because they have big families. They have to take the work because if they don't they lose their dole. Single men and young men like me never get work because we have small dole. We are the ones that need work if the place is to survive."

"Yours is a reasonable viewpoint," the engineer said, "but we have to go by the rules. We cannot give up our right to hire or fire either, or no one will do anything. Above all else we cannot give in to vandals and *scabhaitéirí*."

"I'm one of those vandals you're talking about," McEvilly said. "I'm proud to admit it. I'll go so far as to say that the county council will never get a scheme started on the island if they don't change their policy. I don't want to hold anything up but look at things from my point of view. I cannot get work. I will not be granted a salmon licence. I cannot have a boat other than a currach—there is no safe harbour. We haven't television, or electricity, even toilets. What choice have I but to get out?"

"Unless the love keeps you at home." Jack Phaddy's whisper was clearly heard in the silence that followed Paddy's speech. There was laughter in the hall. Paddy reddened.

"Well if you want to bring love into it, what the hell good is it in a place like this? Who would want to marry and stay in a place that will soon be as empty as the Blaskets?"

There was silence.

Tom Connor then suggested a way around the logjam caused by county council rules. "Is there any reason." he asked, "why you have to do one road at a time? If there is as much money in the kitty as you say, and as much work to be done, why not do them all at the same time and give work to everyone that needs it? As I see it there is enough work to be done to keep everyone able to work employed for years. Don't let some silly little rule hold everything back."

The officials from the county council and the Gaeltacht Department put their heads together. The department official then tentatively asked the assembly, "Would there be any objections or anyone blocking roads if they are all started together, everyone working?" Heads were then put together among the audience. Paddy McEvilly then spoke for the younger men. "If there is fair play for everyone, we're a hundred per cent behind the work being started. And there will be work done too, I guarantee you. We have no objection at all to doing a bit of work." There was a rousing cheer from the hall.

The sea was calm as the officials crossed over in the late evening. Tom Connor, sitting in the prow of one of the currachs, was pleased with the day's work. He was more at ease than he had been in nearly a week. Marion had decided to stay a month at least to give them a chance to think things through properly. There was still a chance, he hoped and prayed—guiltily—that she would lose the baby.

The work on the island roads started on the third Monday in February. Every man who wanted work was given a job. The gangs were carefully drawn up so that people who got on well together would work together.

There was competition between the work gangs, comparisons made each evening in the pub about how much each group had done.

"There'll soon be a road from here to America," Peadar Rua said, "if you were to believe the amount that is being done each day. Hannibal crossing the Alps was not a patch on the lads from this island when it comes to road-building."

The work was hard, the roads being done in the old-fashioned way because of the difficulty of bringing in machinery. Men sat on the road, breaking stones with hammers, filling in on top with sand and gravel.

There were roads being made in the village at the same time, which meant that every able-bodied man in the parish had work. Tom Connor had never seen his parishioners as happy. The Station masses in the houses were held in the evening because of the road-works. Parties followed mass, sometimes until the late hours. Many a thumb got a hammerblow due to hangovers but it was all thought worthwhile.

St Patrick's Day was cold and wet. Tom Connor found the journey from the village to the island as bad as he had ever experienced on the sea. They saw a currach come the other way when they were about half-way across, but could not make out who was in it. Tom had thought no more of it until he went to leave his bag in Jack Phaddy's. The doctor had been there earlier.

Mary had a bad pain during the night. The doctor was sent for, brought by currach in the early morning. He had delivered Mary of a stillborn baby boy. When he got out to the village he was to send for a helicopter to bring Mary to hospital. The island telephone service was out again because of the wind.

"I'm sorry that I won't be able to have any dinner for you, today," was the first thing Mary said when he went back to the room.

"Dinner is the furthest thing from my mind. How are you?"

"As good as can be expected. You heard about the child?"

"Jack told me."

"He's there in the basin under the towel." Tom lifted the cloth, a little red-skinned body of a boy.

"I suppose it's too late to baptise him," she said.

"Do not let that worry you. God is not going to condemn an innocent child."

"Thanks, Tom. I'm glad to hear you say it." She reached for his hand. "God is good." After a little while she said, "This never happened me before. I never had trouble with any of the others. I suppose it's the will of God."

"I don't know. I suppose we cannot blame God for everything."

"I would be the last one to blame him."

"I know that, Mary; it's just that people tend to blame God for every misfortune that befalls them: sometimes we seem to make out that God enjoys seeing people with crosses to carry."

"I might not be able to have any other child."

"Did the doctor say that?" In his own mind he thought, "You would think that ye have enough."

"He didn't say a thing either way."

"Ah, well…with the help of God…The most important thing now is for you to get back to your full health in order to be able to look after the others."

"I only saw Jack for a little while. He is bringing some of the children over to my mother. He was so looking forward to this baby. He will be all right as long as he has something to do. Won't you stay with him tonight? He was doing the Lent on the drink. He might feel like one after this. Anyway it's St Patrick's Day."

"Don't worry about a thing. Jack is as steady as a rock when there is trouble."

"You'll help him with the burial." Her blue eyes filled with tears.

"I will, of course."

Mary kissed his hand, and he nearly went through the ground with shame. He felt so unworthy.

The noise of a helicopter was heard then. By the time Tom reached the door it had landed in a field near the house. Jack was back from his mother-in-law's house in time to help Mary to the helicopter. The medical team was very efficient and fast. Soon the helicopter was nothing more than a dot receding over the horizon.

Tom brought the bigger children for a walk while Jack made the little coffin, two feet long, from white timber. With great care he lined it with a good linen tablecloth and stuffed the lining with wool shearings. When the children came back he explained to them what had happened, showed them the body of their little brother and closed the coffin when they had kissed him.

It was six o'clock with the sun already sinking when they buried the baby in a small grave in a corner of the rocky graveyard, in Mary's father's plot. The priest read the special prayers for such occasions and they walked quietly home together.

When the children had gone to bed, Jack went to the turfstack. As well as an armful of turf he brought a bottle of poteen he had hidden there. He took down two glasses, filled them with the raw whiskey, and they sat one on each side of the fire.

"It's going to be a long night."

"You had it given up for Lent."

"I had, and had intended to keep it up today too, even though I had a drink every St Patrick's Day since I was fifteen years old."

"I suppose it does nothing to cure anything." Tom shook the bottle and watched the little bubbles, "eyes," as people called them, rise steadily in the upturned bottle. "Good stuff, I'd say."

"The best. As you say it doesn't cure anything, but it's badly needed at times. If a person doesn't drown his sorrows sometimes, he is in real danger of drowning himself."

"You were really looking forward to the baby?"

"Both of us were. We like children. What would we be like without them? They help to keep us young, to keep us alive. Maybe there is something else too, that a person is trying to prove that life does not end at forty, that there's life in the old dog yet, that there is a bit of life left in the island."

"There aren't that many signs of life in it yet, though things have improved a bit since we were in Dublin."

"How often have I said that we were the last generation? It takes more than work on the roads to put life in a place. Babies are what are needed."

"There are not that many couples in the place young enough to have children."

"Soon there will be nobody. Unless I am mistaken

that little baby we buried this evening was the last child that will be born on this island in a long time. I would go so far as to say that there is no woman on either side of the parish pregnant at the moment. It is probably the first time this has happened since people populated this side of the country."

Tom looked into the flames, thinking of Marion and the child she was carrying, a child there was no welcome for. "Isn't it strange," he said, "that it is so hard for many people who want children to have them, while people who don't really want them are getting pregnant all the time."

"You would like to have a family yourself?"

"I would, if I was married. I am not so sure about the one that's on the way now. Marion is pregnant, Jack."

It took the news a while to sink in; "Jesus, Tom, I don't know what to say. It's not that I thought you were a living saint, that ye mightn't sleep together...I never expected this would happen."

"It has happened, and we don't know what to do about it."

"Is there any need to tell anyone? Didn't many the girl go away and have a baby, and no one was any the wiser."

"It's not what people know or what they think that counts in the long run, Jack. It's part of ourselves, just as the child you buried today was part of yourself and Mary. That's why it's so hard to give it up."

"Don't I know."

"That's what I was thinking this evening when you were putting your little boy in the ground."

"There's no way you can have the baby and be a priest at the same time?"

"I'm sure the authorities would expect Marion to go, both of us to go, if it comes to that. If not, they would probably just dismiss me as a priest of the diocese. At the same time I feel that if people here came to accept it, that they would still accept me as their priest, there might be a chance the bishop would give in."

"I don't know is there a bishop in the world would accept that. He himself would surely get short shrift from the Pope."

"It does not happen often in this country. There is often a blind eye turned to it in other countries."

"If there is we don't get to hear much about it. When you think about it, I suppose you don't have a lot to lose if you do stay on. If you have to go, there is not much difference between going of your own free will, and being driven out. If you have any chance at all to stay on, stay. Here's one person—and I'm sure Mary too—that's willing to stand by you."

"I wouldn't like to do anything at the same time that would harm the faith of the people."

"If the people's faith cannot take that much, it's not worth their while to have faith."

"You might be right."

"I am right. The people's faith would put up with anything. If the Pope of Rome and the Queen of England had twins tomorrow, it would not affect the faith of the people other than by causing a pleasant little divarsion for the gossip-mongers for a day or two. As far as I can see the only thing that affects people's faith is not having any challenge, sailing before the wind all the time."

"If everyone looked at things or thought about

things the way you do…"

"To tell you the truth, Tom Connor, I don't know if it's the faith of the people that's worrying you at all but what they will think about yourself, the lovely man, the kind priest, that they never had the likes of before."

"Maybe there is truth in what you are saying. The person himself is often the last one to see his own faults. I know for sure that it would be difficult to live in a place like this without the support, the backing, the approval of the people."

"That's fair enough. But if that is the reason for not following your conscience, you are not much of a man. I do not think you are a weak character. I think there is a lot more to you than you have found out about yourself yet, and I hope that you stay on and prove it."

"Going or staying, I'm glad to have got to know yourself and Mary. I hope we continue to be friends, whatever happens."

"Leave it there. Shake on that." The glasses were emptied. "We had better eat something or I'll be dying in the morning and I won't be able to get those children out to school."

Jack took half a chicken from the larder. They had eaten nothing all day, and sat at the table, tearing apart the carcase of the chicken and eating it. They threw the bones in the fire.

"Celibate spat," Jack mused. "Who would think that the last generation in this parish would come from celibate spat? I always knew you had it in you, Connor. May you be the father of a bishop."

The harmony caused by the fact that all the island men were working did not last very long. A batch of letters arrived from a solicitor which were to fan the flames of jealousy and disharmony again. Everybody related to Bridgie Hughie got a letter asking them were they willing to renounce any claim they had to her property.

Bridgie had made a will about ten years before in which she had left her house and land to Patcheen John, on condition that he looked after her as long as she lived. She was sick at the time, and Patcheen had asked a visiting priest to draw up the will, as well as anointing her. He drafted the will as best he could, and advised Patcheen to bring it to a solicitor to check had he written the will correctly, and gone through all the proper procedures. With the will in his pocket Patcheen decided to leave well enough alone and not show it to anyone.

When Bridgie died Patcheen brought the will into a solicitor in the city to have the land transferred in his own name. The solicitor noticed immediately that there was a flaw in the will. It was not stated that the witnesses signed in the presence of each other. There would have been no problem if the witnesses were alive and could verify that they had signed in each other's presence. Both had died in the intervening years. Even the priest who drew up the will could not be found. He had left the order and was reputedly married in Canada. His superiors had no record of a forwarding address.

When the solicitor asked Patcheen for permission to go ahead and have the will proven, Patcheen did not fully understand the implications. "What do you want permission for?" he said, "Isn't that what I'm paying you to do."

When people who were distant relatives of Bridgie got letters asking them to renounce any rights they had to her property they were most surprised. They had no wish or intention to take the land away from Patcheen but there was no way that they were going to renounce their rights to anything. At first each thought it was only they that had got the letter. Gradually word filtered back from the United States that people there had got them too. Patcheen was sure that there was a conspiracy to take the land from him and that it was Jack Phaddy that was behind it. To gain his revenge he wrote to the unemployment exchange informing them that Jack was earning money from seaweed as well as drawing the dole.

There was little work done on the island during Holy Week, and especially in the last three days. People had great devotion to the passion of Christ. On Good Friday, men who were never seen near the altar at any other time braved the aisle to kiss the cross of Christ, the poor man's communion as someone had called it.

For the first time in quite a few years Paddy McEvilly was among them. Barbara had asked him to go. He did not know what to make of her, she seemed to have changed so much since Christmas. She had come home at Easter a born saint, confession, communion, ceremonies, hints that she was thinking of joining the convent.

He had visited her on a number of occasions during the previous term, pretending that he was her brother. He knew from the nun's knowing smile that they were used to that kind of "brother," the kind that fell from the sky during the Christmas holidays. They had lovely walks together in the convent garden, Barbara the same lively, loving girl he had got to know during the Christmas break. But since she came home at Easter he was almost afraid to hold her hand, she acted the little saint so well.

"You don't seem to like me any more," she said to him on Easter Saturday night as they walked down the road together after the Resurrection mass. Paddy had come over on the turn with the priest on Thursday and was staying with friends in the village for the weekend.

"What makes you think that? Of course I like you. What would I be doing here if I did not?"

"I don't have any contagious disease."

"Disease?"

"There must be something wrong with me when you are afraid to put your arm around me, or give me a kiss."

"You don't give me much of a chance. I don't like to go too close to you when you're going around like a nun."

Barbara burst out laughing. "Me, like a nun. If the real nuns in the convent were to hear you they would have a great laugh."

"I don't think it's a strange thing to say at all. You have hardly left the chapel since you came home, and on top of that you're making me go as well."

"A bit of religion would do you no harm at all."

"Well, the prayers are over now until tomorrow morning. Is there any hope at all of a kiss?"

They made up for lost time, standing in the dark in the middle of the road. When they paused to draw breath, Barbara asked, "What are you going to do for the rest of the night?"

"Guess."

"You dirty old man. Do men ever think of anything else?"

"I didn't say anything. All I want is to be with you, in your company, if you want it spelled out."

"You're no good at all to me so, or any other woman either. Your poor wife is going to be frozen in the bed."

"Not while I'm around. What's the point in talking about the night when Pádraic Mhichilín expects you home at midnight?"

"There's a way around that. There's a window in the room."

"Do you think I'm out of my mind? If your old man caught me…I thought you said your sister was in the room with you."

"Teresa. She is, but I'm not talking of you going in but of me coming out."

"And what will we do then?"

"It's my turn to ask—guess?"

"You're impossible."

"We could do what the tourists do—go up to the old castle and have a bit of a barbecue, roast a couple of rashers on a fire. Tigh Sheoinín is still open. You could go and get a six-pack and a packet of rashers while I'm gone in home."

"I wouldn't be surprised but that you have this planned for ages."

Cáit and Pádraic Mhichilín, as well as Teresa, were already in bed. Barbara made plenty of noise with the bolt of the door before going to her parents' door to call out "Goodnight." She quenched the lamp in the kitchen and went into her bedroom. Teresa was peacefully asleep. She opened the bottom half of the window when Paddy knocked quietly. He had bought the party stuff, as well as rejecting a number of offers of drinks in Tigh Sheoinín.

"Come on in," Barbara whispered jokingly when she had the window raised.

"You must be out of your mind."

"Here, pull my arm. I'll never get out in that small space."

She stood on a chair, putting her head and shoulders out through the window. She had a fit of giggles when Paddy cupped her breast and whispered—"I'll get a good grip on this." He turned his back to the window, she put her arms around his shoulders, and he pulled her, piggyback style, through the opening.

"Ssssh, cut out the skitting," Paddy warned, "or your father will be out after us."

The window was stuck in an open position. It came down with a bang when Paddy forced it. They waited for a reaction from inside the house. "Come on," Barbara said. "There's always something banging in the wind."

Barbara carried the plastic bag, Paddy an armful of turf from Pádraic Mhichilín's turfstack.

The castle was roofless itself but there was a cellar underneath. Cattle sometimes sheltered there in the winter, and it was a well-known courting haunt in summertime. It took Paddy a while to light the turf because there was neither a hearth nor a chimney in the place. The cellar was full of smoke for a while but it cleared gradually through the doorway. They burned the bacon when the fire got too hot but there was a lovely smell from it and what could be eaten was delicious.

"Who is going to wash the dishes?" Paddy asked.

"Isn't it great when the only washing to be done is licking your fingers. That is the way people should always eat."

"You're not very fond of washing up."

"I hate it."

"What will you do when you get married?"

"I'll marry a man that will do them for me, at least share them."

"And who will that lucky man be?"

"A girl has to wait until she is asked."

"Not in this day and age. A woman liberated enough to marry a dishwasher wouldn't wait to be asked."

"Do you want me to announce my choice now?"

"You're too young to be talking of marriage yet."

"I'm seventeen. I'll soon have my Leaving Cert."

"Isn't it you that's sure of yourself."

"My head is not as empty as you think."

"Seventeen is very young."

"Same age as my mother was."

"You'll take off like the rest of them as soon as school is finished."

"A year ago, six months ago, that was what I had in mind."

"And now?"

"You know as well as I do. I want to be with you."

Paddy did not say anything for a while.

"That is what I would want too…"

"But…"

"I'm not sure that you know what you would be letting yourself in for. This place is quiet enough, but the island."

"I would put up with anything as long as I was with

you."

"What about the middle of winter? Remember that you have not spent a winter here since you were twelve. You only see what the place is like in summer and the other holidays."

"That is true, but that is the kind of talk that has left the place like it is, full of bachelors that thought it was too much to ask a young woman to stay. Do you know what I learned at Christmas? My two sisters in America would give an arm and a leg for the chance to stay and marry and raise a family around here. They loved the States when they were younger. They are fed up now with crime, and being afraid to go out at night, being afraid even when they are in their apartment. I have no doubt but that they will marry over there but it's only because the men here haven't the guts to ask them."

"They be so done up and painted and powdered that the lads here wouldn't think themselves good enough for them. They would be afraid to touch them in case they would break, like expensive dolls." Barbara laughed.

"If they heard you—Pádraic Mhichilín's daughters. It's true for me though. There's many the girl that would stay if she got a bit of encouragement, if the men had a bit of guts in them. But ye prefer to be hanging on to your mothers' skirts."

"How would things be in a few years when a girl would be regretting not having gone to university?"

"Once she would be qualified she could go at any time."

"With a couple of children under her *ascal*."

"He could look after the children for a few years. I'm not the silly little bitch you think I am. I would never consider coming back to stay here if I did not know what is involved. I was born and reared here. I was brought up with a sister that is different. I know a little bit about hardship. I would be near my parents."

"I wouldn't want my little woman running home to mammy every five minutes."

Barbara was ready to explode when she saw that Paddy was joking. Her own laugh came to an abrupt end when she thought she heard something. "Paddy, do you believe in ghosts?"

"Ghosts. What have ghosts to do with it?"

At this stage Pádraic Mhichilín realised he had been seen so he entered the cellar. The noise of the window closing had aroused him and he had got up to investigate. When he discovered that Barbara was no longer in the house he headed for the castle. He guessed correctly that she would be where he and Cáit had done their own courting.

"Is this what they are teaching you in the convent? Teaching you to deceive your father and mother? And you, you would think you would stay where you come from, instead of coming over here to seduce little girls…" He ran out of words. He had never been much good at giving out.

"What are we doing that's so wrong?" Paddy spread his hands, shrugging his shoulders in the same movement.

"You keep a grip to your tongue, *a mhac*. I should send for the guards, giving drink to a girl under eighteen."

"Didn't the doctor recommend that she drink Guinness."

"You stay away from her from now on."

"I want to marry her."

"Marry…What have you to offer any woman?"

"The same as you had, a bit of land, a house."

"If I ever see you around here again…"

Paddy walked quietly out. Barbara looked at him with an eye that could melt someone. But what was he supposed to do? Hit her father?

All Pádraic said to his daughter on the way home was, "Your mother will have something to say to you tomorrow."

Cáit was sitting up in bed when they returned. She had been worried, but she laughed when he told her what he had found in the castle cellar. "Is that all?" she said. "There mustn't be too much harm in the poor man. When you were his age it wasn't eating rashers you used to be."

"Is that all you have to say about your daughter sneaking off in the middle of the night with that rascal from the island?"

"I think it is very wrong of her to deceive us and I will be talking to her about that tomorrow. But I've nothing against her going out with a lad from the island. We can't be after her all the time. The others were in America at sixteen and we didn't know what they were doing or who they were with."

"That school isn't doing her much good. A waste of time and money, I'd say," Pádraic said as he loosened his boots.

"Thank God it's not costing us anything. The biggest fault I had with the school was that it was educating them to go away, that we would soon have no one left except Teresa."

"There is nothing here for anyone in this day and

age."

"This might be the answer to our prayers," Cáit mused aloud to herself. "If she was to marry locally, she would look after Teresa when we're gone. That always worried me."

"It might be the answer to your prayers... That fellow is as wild as a March hare."

"Every one of those McEvillys was nice. I was listening to this fellow on the radio that time they were up in Dublin. I'd say he is a lad that has spunk in him."

"But Barbara is so young."

"You married a girl nearly as young. Are you saying now that you regret it?"

"No, but..."

"They are not talking of getting married today or tomorrow. Give them time and see how things work out."

"I suppose you would give them the place too."

"Whoever looks after Teresa should get the place. Anyway hasn't Paddy McEvilly a place of his own."

"Did we say the prayers yet?" Pádraic changed the subject, as he climbed into bed. The women always had the last word.

Patcheen John's cattle were found wandering twice during Easter. They had broken out of part of Bridgie Hughie's holding. It was not clear how the gap had opened, was the wall knocked maliciously or had the cattle breasted it down? A heifer was in heat, and it was quite possible that she had broken out and that the other cattle followed. Patcheen himself had no doubt but that it was Jack Phaddy that had let them out. He brought his brother-in-law, Paddy McEvilly, with him to sit and wait all night, and with luck catch the villain.

"I don't believe that there is anyone knocking the gap," Paddy said. "It's that bitch of a heifer. If you let the bull at her he would soon quieten her down."

"She's too young. She would be too small at the turn of the year to have a calf. That Hereford bull gives them very big heads."

Although they were well clothed, the cold got to them increasingly as the night went on. Patcheen's fingers were nearly frozen to the double barrels of his shotgun. He had accused Jack Phaddy in the pub the night before of letting out his cattle.

"I didn't leave a hand on any wall belonging to you," Jack had said. "I came in here for a quiet pint, so don't be disturbing me like a good man. Bridgie's land is going to your head altogether."

"You stay away from my land."

"Your land." Jack could never resist the chance of a dig. "You mean Bridgie Hughie's land?"

"Yeah. It's my land now."

"It seems that land is a kind of commonage now. According to the letters that solicitor sent out we all have a claim to it."

Patcheen was fit to be tied. He vowed revenge on Jack Phaddy. "Wait until the gauger catches up with him," he said to Paddy, as they waited in the dark. "The gauger will give him his come-uppance."

"The gauger won't bother Jack."

"He will, when he reads the report I sent in on him, making his fortune on seaweed and signing on while the rest of us are working."

"What kind of a fucking cunt are you, spying on your neighbour, a man that had to give up work on the roads when his wife lost a baby? I am not the greatest admirer Jack Phaddy has but I wouldn't inform on anyone."

"I won't let him make a fool out of me."

They heard the noise of a wall falling. Patcheen fired both barrels in the air. He was not going to risk shooting his cattle.

"What kind of *amadán* are you?" Paddy said. "You have thrown away whatever chance there was of catching somebody, that is if there was somebody."

"Didn't you hear the stones falling. I'll bet you that is the last wall that will be knocked on me. Come on, and we'll teach Jack Phaddy a lesson."

"With a gun?"

"I'm not that stupid. We will give him a taste of his own medicine. We'll knock enough walls on him that will keep him building for a week."

"I'll have nothing to do with that."

"What's wrong with you? You're getting as soft as shit. That girl of Pádraic Mhichilín's has you ruined."

It was a grey day in April and the daffodils were dying when Tom Connor announced at mass on the island that Marion was expecting a baby and that he was the father. They had discussed the matter together a thousand times since the beginning of the year. On Easter Sunday they had decided finally to stay together whatever the consequences and that it was time for him to tell the parishioners. People were already telling Marion that she was putting on weight. He would inform the bishop when he had informed the people.

Tom Connor never heard the congregation as quiet as when he informed them that they would soon have another reason to call him "Father." He had a letter in the post to the bishop, he said, a letter a lot depended on. If he had to leave the parish—which he probably would—he wanted to thank them for their help and kindnesses over the years.

They had decided to stay together to rear their child, he said, because they believed people should be responsible for their actions. If he did not have to leave the priesthood, he would like to have their permission to remain on as their priest. It was asking a lot, he knew; it all depended on the bishop, of course.

Bridgie Hughie's land, the main topic of conversation until then, was quickly forgotten. People did not know what to say. They had never been confronted with a situation like this before. Some immediately blamed Marion, this woman who had come and "seduced the holy priest."

"The bitch, the *straoil*, wherever she came from," Mary Guiney said to her next-door neighbour, Bríd McEvilly, on the way home from mass, "who stole the priest of God from us. There was a time the likes of her would be burned to death and it wouldn't be half good enough for her. To think that we had to accept the holy communion from hands like his, sinful hands."

"Sure it was always said—do what they say, not what they do. When you think about it, what is it but human nature taking its course. Isn't it a lonesome life too for a young person."

"If he wasn't fit for it he should have stayed away from the priesthood. I never thought, Bríd, that I'd find you standing up for a Judas like that. A millstone should be hung about his neck and be drowned in the depths of the sea."

"The same Lord said, 'Judge not so that you may not be judged.' "

"Hell's fire for eternity isn't long enough."

"The poor creature was kind. I suppose there is not much chance the bishop will leave him to us now."

"If he does, I'm going to change my religion."

"What good would that do? Don't Protestant ministers have wives and children too?"

Most people did not discuss the matter at all. It was not the kind of thing people talked about in front of the children, or even with other adults. People had plenty of experience of sexual innuendo and double talk. It was something else to talk seriously about it in public. The pubs were quieter than usual. People may have felt let down or betrayed but they kept their own counsel. Jack Jennings made a few attempts to raise it with his customers, but he got few answers other than "yes" and "no."

"The silence is worse than if people came and burned down the house over our heads," Marion said the following evening. "We don't know what people are saying or thinking. Neither of us has spoken to anyone since you made your announcement. Is there a boycott on us or what?"

"The very same crowd as usual were at daily mass this morning. There was no boycott on that anyway."

"They must still accept you as a priest so. What are we going to do when we run out of groceries? I have no notion of walking into Jack Jennings. I heard he refused to serve an unmarried mother in years gone by."

"Soon enough we will find out one way or the other."

"It's a wonder the bishop has not been on to you."

"He wouldn't have my letter until tomorrow at the earliest. The post only goes every second day—in the bus."

"It's a wonder Jennings has not been on to him."

A phone-call from the bishop's secretary, Peter Gilmore, proved that Jack Jennings had indeed been to the city that day and visited Bishop Caufield. Tom was asked to report immediately to "Bishop's House." They did not call it a palace any more.

"Thanks be to God something is happening," Marion said. "I was ready for anything, from murder down, everything except this awful silence."

Something happened that evening that caused the meeting with the bishop to be postponed and gave people a different cause for sorrow. Mick Macken was found hanging in his own barn, an event that shocked the community far more than the priest's dramatic sermon the previous Sunday.

Mick had been highly respected as an oarsman, a tradesman, and as a big, kind, gentle soul that never refused help to anyone. It was clear for some time that there had been something wrong. He took no care of his appearance, went about in ragged clothes, unshaven and dirty. No one knew where he got the poteen but it was obvious that he was drinking heavily. His cow had been heard a couple of nights lowing painfully because she had not been milked.

Mick's condition caused his old friend Pádraic Mhichilín a lot of concern and worry. On that Monday evening he set out to visit him, a six-pack of Guinness under his arm. He had meant to call the previous day— it was not like Mick to miss Sunday mass—but he had been so upset by the priest's sermon, he could not talk to anyone. He found Mick's house neat and clean, everything in its place. When Mick himself was not in he looked in the barn...

There was a big funeral that clear April day. Half of the island people had crossed over to pay their respects. Tom Connor preached on the scripture: "Her sins, her many sins have been forgiven, because she loved much," thinking of himself as much as, or more than, Mick Macken. He was buried in the deep sandy village graveyard that was such a contrast to the island cemetery. Mick was the last of another village family. In fifty years more would there be anyone left?

Paddy McEvilly got a surprise when Pádraic Mhichilín invited him for a drink. He had not seen Barbara since that night in the castle, and he was wary of Pádraic. It was as if nothing had happened, Pádraic talking about everything under the sun except his daughter.

"You've really done it this time." The bishop did not even look at Tom when he entered the room. "You gave me nothing but trouble since the day you were ordained. I put up with a lot...I'm a patient man. I would take even more, such as the gratuitous public insults you have so often given me; but public scandal— that is more than I am prepared to take."

He sat behind the big oak table, his voice shivering with emotion. "It is a real pity, because despite your attitude to authority and to me personally, I believe that you were a good priest in your own way. You were kind to your parishioners. I hear you were extremely good to the old and the sick. You stood up for the rights of the people. Even if I did not personally agree with everything you did, I know that you were a good priest, and I will be very sad to lose you from the diocese."

"I am very grateful for what you have just said."

"You will, of course, leave as quietly as is now possible. Enough harm has already been done, but I understand that you were under pressure and could not see any other way out. There should not be any difficulty in getting a quick laicisation, so that you can marry. Even the present Holy Father has laicised priests in situations like this when there is danger of scandalising the faithful. Even he gives in, as it were, to the shotgun." The bishop gave an embarrassed laugh.

"But I do not want to get married. And I do not want to leave the priesthood."

"You do not..." David Caufield looked at Tom Connor in the eyes for the first time since the meeting began. "You do not want... You have no other choice. You are not so stupid as to think that you can remain a priest of this diocese after all that has happened. What about the girl? Do you not think there is a need to do 'the right thing' with regard to your 'friend?' "

"I am not going to let Marion down, if that is what you mean, but she does not want to marry formally either nor does she want me to leave the priesthood. I personally do not see why I have to turn my back on my vocation because of a mistake. Would it not be a more Christian thing to accept responsibility for our actions than to run away from them? You would think that the biggest punishment would be to let me carry this cross as it were, to show a person has to be responsible for his actions, even if this draws the opprobrium of the people on him."

"It might be acceptable to talk like that if people looked on it like that. But that it not the way people would look at it, they would see it as *carte blanche* to do whatever you like. As in the old legend of the *gobán saor*, you would have the skin and its price, '*an craiceann agus an luach*.'"

"Now that you mention *craiceann*—it has a sexual connotation as you know in the Gaeltacht. If it goes to that I am not the only clergyman to have the *craiceann* and the *luach*. The others manage—and good luck to them—not to get caught. There is no sin really in this Church other than getting caught. But if I have to leave the priesthood, there are many priests and bishops that will have questions to answer about their own relationships with women. These are men no different from me, apart from the fact that they are smarter. They don't make mistakes. They don't get caught."

"There is nothing wrong in having a woman friend— the Lord himself had—there is nothing wrong even for a priest to fall in love so long as it stays like that, platonic love."

"I read a lot of Plato in my time, David. You could go so far as to say I was one of the last of the Greeks—as far as study is concerned anyway—in this country. Platonic love gives me even more scope than you think I have had."

"I mean platonic in the accepted sense of the word."

"That's lovely—if you are a saint. All that I'm saying is that media people might like to investigate why you yourself, for example, brought that beautiful secretary/ housekeeper/whatever with you from the parish when you were made bishop."

"The simple answer is that she can be trusted. She is very good at her job."

"I'm sure she is, David. I'm sure she is. I would not dare to suggest otherwise. It just might look strange to the media that she lives here with you, while I apparently have to leave the priesthood because of a natural, human—call it 'sin' if you like. They might think that there is no difference between us except that I got caught."

"Yourself and your 'sin if you like.' Not to speak of your attempted blackmail." David Caufield was really angry. "What kind of a sin is a 'sin if you like?' I suppose that when you're saying mass, you say, 'Lamb of God who takes away the "sins if you like" of the world.' What you call 'sin if you like' I call sacrilege. You have some neck to come in here trying to lecture me, after causing a public scandal to the faithful."

"All I'm saying is that I am not prepared to leave the priesthood or to be thrown out of it without question. My conscience would not allow it."

"Conscience...Where was your conscience when you were with her?"

"My conscience tells me to be answerable for what I do. It does not tell me to leave the priesthood."

"Most people would think it was the same thing."

"I cannot leave without raising some questions about all this. Why should I when there are bishops and priests and cardinals getting away with the same thing?"

"If it is so important to you to stay in the priesthood, why does she not give the baby for adoption. You could go on the missions, or something."

"That child is part of ourselves. It is Marion and I that created this child. We want to be responsible for it."

"It was a great mistake for me to send you to that place the first day. You've completely lost your reason."

"What would Christ do in a case like this?"

"Now, Tom. Leave Christ out of this."

"That is the trouble with this Church. Christ is left out of it."

"That is nice talk from an...Antichrist..." The bishop sat back in his chair with his hands in front of his face. His body sagged, as if he had lost all control of it. After a long time, he said: "I'm sorry for saying that. Why can we not discuss it in a civilised way? Do you know what I want you to do? Take a fortnight. Do a retreat or something. Do not go back to the parish, please. I will have a decision for you when you return. You will have to accept my decision. And Tom..."

"Yes?"

"Pray. Pray for both of us."

Jack Phaddy was on the look-out for the gauger for some time. He had heard on the grapevine that Patcheen John had reported him for gathering and selling seaweed, and drawing dole at the same time. Because Mary lost the baby Jack had not gone back working on the road after St Patrick's Day.

Mary was depressed since she returned from the hospital. She had no desire, no incentive, to rise in the morning, no interest in doing anything during the day. She often spent whole days crying. She had lost interest in how she looked, and despite her love for the children she felt as if they were nothing but a burden to her. Jack was thoughtful and considerate, something which drove her mad altogether. He had not had a drink since St Patrick's Day, the day she lost the baby. She was upset too about Tom Connor and Marion. She did not like it, whatever Jack said about human nature. It was against the faith as she understood it. But when a strange priest came to say the Sunday mass in Tom's place, she forgave everything—she wanted Tom to stay. Mick Macken's death depressed her too. She felt she understood why he did what he did. The weight of the world was down on her, she felt.

When Jack heard that the gauger had been in the village the previous week looking for someone to take him across in a currach, he made his plans. The inspector of the unemployed had been told the weather was not suitable for a crossing but there would be no excuse when a fine day came.

"Are you out of your mind?" Mary said when he told her his plan. "I'm hardly able to rise from my bed, never mind getting involved in that kind of carry-on."

"We have to do something or the dole will be cut back on us. We're finding it hard enough as it is."

"Get someone else, Jack. I wouldn't be up to it."

"It would do you good."

"How is that?"

"You need some kind of interest to bring you back to yourself."

"I can't help it." Mary started to cry.

Jack put his arms around her. "I know well that you cannot help it but you need something to get you out of the depression."

"That's the word for it. I don't know what's wrong with me. It's like a big black cloud down on top of me."

"I understand how you feel. It's often the same kind

of feeling drove me to drink. I think this plan will be a bit of help in getting you over it. It will be a bit of crack if nothing else."

"Crack is the farthest thing from my mind. You're very good to me, Jack, this last few weeks. I don't know what I would have done except for all the help with the children and the house." The tears rolled down from her eyes again.

"Don't you know that I love you and hate to see you under that big black cloud of sadness."

"I'm sorry Jack... I..." His kiss interrupted her. "Ah, Jack." Jack lay on the bed beside her, held her in his arms. "Margaret won't be awake for an hour yet—the others are at school."

Mary laughed; "You're beginning to sound like your man that was on holidays a couple of years ago, asking the girls, 'I suppose a ride is out of the question.'"

"It's nice to see you laugh again."

When Margaret woke them an hour later, Mary was feeling better. She agreed to help Jack out with his plan.

When the gauger did arrive on the island more than a week later Mary was back to her old self. They had enjoyed rehearsing what they were going to do when he came. When news arrived that there was a stranger coming across in a currach, Mary had a drink of brandy to settle her nerves. Jack went to the back kitchen when they saw a man with a brief-case under his arm come up the road.

Mary had squeezed herself into a mini-dress she had not worn since their honeymoon twelve years before, a time when short skirts were all the rage. She was a fair deal heavier now and in danger of exploding through the dress at any moment. She had liberally sprayed herself and the kitchen with perfume, and sat deep in the sofa, one bare knee across the other, a glass of brandy in one hand, a cigarette in the other.

"Come in." There was so much leg, thigh and breast to be seen that the official did not know where to look.

"Excuse me, is the man of the house in?"

"He's not here at the moment."

"Where would I find him?"

"The best thing you could do is stay here until he comes back."

"I would only be in your way."

"You would not, *a stór*. This place is so lonely that we're delighted when any holidaymaker calls." She moved over to make room on the couch. "Take the weight off your feet."

"Thanks." He sat on one of the chairs.

"I'll get you a cup of tea."

"No thanks, I'm fine."

"You would prefer a drink?"

"I never drink when I'm working."

"Whiskey or brandy?"

"Neither, thanks."

"You're only saying that. You're very shy, *a mhaicín*." Her boldness surprised herself. She did not know where she was getting the banter from. How long could she keep it up?

"You must be cold after the crossing. A little drop of brandy will heat you up. You won't know yourself."

"No, thanks…Please."

"Make yourself at home. You look like a lad that would drink the cross of an ass, if he wasn't so shy."

She brought over a glass of brandy and spilled half of it on top of the visitor, as if accidentally. "Sorry, *a mhaicín*. Wait until I dry you." She made as if to mop the front of his trousers with a little handkerchief."

"What is going on here?" Jack fought hard with himself to keep in the laughter. Mary looked funnier than the gauger.

"Excuse me…" He stood up, and pushed Mary, still pretending to dry his clothes, away.

"You had better have a very good excuse. I presume you are a doctor. We have no milkmen here. According to the English papers the milkman is the most common rake in the business. Window-cleaners too, I'm led to believe."

"You know damn well that this is all a set-up."

"There will be a right set-up unless you have a very good excuse or explanation."

"I'm the inspector from the labour exchange."

"I don't mind what kind of an inspector you are. You have no right to inspect my wife."

"My office has been made aware that you have been earning money from the sale of seaweed while continuing to avail of unemployment assistance. I was sent out to carry out an investigation."

"I have not finished my own investigation yet. What were you doing to my wife when I came in just now?" He turned to Mary, afraid she would burst out laughing. "Go back to the room and put on some decent clothes. I'll deal with you later."

"It's as plain as a pikestaff that you are both trying to work the head on me. But that will not work. I have my job to do."

"It wasn't your head you were trying to work, you lousy gauger."

The official backed away around the table as Jack

approached menacingly. "If I take you to court, it will be only your word against Mary's and mine."

"You wouldn't stoop...."

"Get the hell out of this house and this island while the going is good."

"I have my work to do. When word comes in, I have to carry out an investigation."

"I have to stand up for my rights too. Why do you accept and act on anonymous letters? I'll accept an investigation if you bring the person who informed on me here or to some sort of court. They should be made to back up their malicious information."

"I only do the job I'm paid to do."

"I think the likes of you have taken over from the landlords' bailiffs of the last century as the scourge of the poor people. Here I find you pawing my wife as well. You'll soon be looking to sleep the first night with newly-married women, like the agents long ago. Well, I intend to protect my wife and my children, one way or another. It has got to the stage of self-defence. Do you understand that, gauger? Self-defence. It was very big in the catechism in my time, something that gave you permission to do anything in your own defence, murder, if it comes to that. You are allowed to defend your own and your livelihood. Do you understand what I'm saying?"

"Listen to me. I think you're going over the top altogether."

"You, listen to me in my house. As I see it, it is self-defence to put up a fight to keep your dole. It is the only livelihood we have out here. If I make a few pound on seaweed, what's the loss to the government? Doesn't it keep a factory going somewhere? Is it not better for me and my wife and my family and my country to be out doing something than to be sitting on my arse, or on a high stool in the pub all day?"

"Listen, a minute..."

"You listen. I have no doubt that it costs the taxpayer more to keep you on the road harassing the likes of me, than the couple of lousy shillings they save from cutting back dole. Well, the people of this place are not willing to take much more. We have picketed the Dáil already, and we won't stop there in our efforts to gain our rights. No one will walk on us any more."

"I'm not trying to walk on you. Look, I understand your case. There will be no clawback on your income but there was no need to try to trick or intimidate me. That is a very dangerous thing to do to a government official. I will not take it any further this time. Do not try it on again."

"It's all we have."

"I know. Does the offer of that glass of brandy still stand?"

Barbara was delighted when Sister Bríd said that her brother was waiting for her in the visitors' room. Paddy, at last. She had not seen him since Easter. She had feared that she might never see him again. She had been vexed with him that night in the castle, letting her father lead her away by the hand like a child. He had not crossed again from the island despite the fact that she still had a week's holiday left at the time.

She had pretended to herself that she did not care, that she was better off without him, but she had not been able to fool herself. She spent the week after Easter at home, bitching and biting, refusing to eat, staying in her room with a "puss" on her. All her mother had said about that Saturday night was, "You would think we would be able to trust each other." It drove her mad altogether that they were so nice to her, they must be confident, she felt, now that Paddy had been driven away from her. She would show them all. She would work hard for the last term, get a good Leaving Cert. That would be her ticket out of the place, away from her father and her mother, away from Teresa, from McEvilly and everything belonging to him. As long as she lived she would not let any other man break her heart.

As she walked down the corridor towards the visitors' room, she had in mind to give him a piece of her mind but when she saw him standing there awkwardly among the polished pieces of furniture, her heart leaped with joy. She ran over to him. She hugged, she kissed him. Then she started to cry.

"Paddy, Paddy, Paddy," she said between kisses, "Why have you stayed away from me for so long?"

"Wasn't I working every day?"

"Work was more important than me."

"A person cannot live on love."

"Even one day off."

"There has not been work available on the island for five years. I complained about that more than most. If I was taking days off when there is work they would say McEvilly was good for nothing but talk."

"And they might be right."

"Why would they?"

"I'm really vexed with you."

"You would never think it from the way you kissed me."

"You didn't stand up to my father that night."

"Did you expect me to hit him, or what?"

"No, but…"

"What else could I do?"

"I don't know. Oh, I'm so happy that you came to see me."

"Isn't it me that's charitable."

"You are, to yourself. Come on. You have to get permission to bring me out to town."

"I asked already. I am allowed take you for a cup of tea." He tried to put on a fancy accent.

"Tea? Vodka, more likely!"

"Oh, the youth of today."

"It was you led me astray, in your ould barn."

"It was easy lead you astray, if I remember correctly. Are you doing much study?"

"I never worked so hard in my life—trying to forget you."

"You'll be too grand for us before long, Leaving Cert and university, I suppose."

"If I don't get any better offers."

"That's what brought me here today."

"You're joking."

"Will you marry me during the summer?"

"You're serious?"

"If you're willing to take a chance on life with me, why wait?"

"Is it as simple as that? You cannot marry before you're twenty-one without the permission of your parents."

"If they don't give permission can't you come to live with me. That will soon change their minds."

"My mother would really love that."

"I'm sure she would. I would be surprised if it came to that. I had a drink with your father at Mick Macken's funeral. He was very nice altogether to me. I think they cannot wait for me to take you off their hands."

"Maybe you'll want to get rid of me just as quickly."

"It doesn't matter too much to me married or single so long as we can be together."

"The priest and everyone would be down on us."

"Wasn't the priest himself....You heard about that?"

"The nuns said prayers for a priest gone astray. All the girls in the place had the gossip. What do they think at home?"

"Nobody is saying very much. They don't like to see Connor having to go, if he has to. Isn't it their own business anyways. As far as I'm concerned the Church is rotten from top to bottom."

"You can't be saying things like that about the Church when we get married. I'm a good Catholic, I want you to know."

"I'm delighted to hear it. We will have a houseful of children."

"We will, if you have them. I'm going to have two, a boy and a girl."

"Five."

"Three, so."

"Split the difference. Four."

"Whatever you say, Daddy."

"There won't be any if you're as cold as you were at Easter."

"Cold? Me, cold?"

"You were so holy."

"That's not allowed until after you're married."

"What's wrong with a bit of practice?"

"I hope the nuns are not listening to you."

"Maybe they are at it too. That one that brought me in here looked gamey enough."

"Bríd? She's nice. It's a pity they are not all like her. But it's no wonder some of them are so cranky, the life they have. It's really tough."

"That one knew well I was not your brother."

"Bríd understands the crack as good as ourselves."

"Come on out the town, and we'll have a look at a few rings."

"I didn't say I would marry you yet."

"You'll do what you're told from now on."

"You must be...you are joking."

Bishop Caufield asked his secretary, Father Peter Gilmore, to do the duties of Father Connor the first weekend in May. Apart from the usual priestly duties he was to prepare a report on what people felt about "the recent scandal."

"Talk to the schoolteachers and the shopkeepers, young people too, of course, but it is the viewpoint of good staunch Catholics I want most. Priests visit the old and sick with holy communion on the first Friday of the month. This will give you an opportunity to get into quite a few houses, and suss out what the people are thinking."

Father Gilmore was a big strong man who looked a lot younger than his forty-eight years, athletic, without a grey rib in his handsome head. He had been considered the power behind the throne of the previous bishop, when the old man was verging on senility. Many thought he would be a shoo-in for the position when old Maughan passed away. Rome had other ideas, the chief one being David Caufield. He had kept Gilmore on as an organiser, sorter-out of problems, and, it was said, in order to keep a potential rival on a short lead.

Old Jack Jennings gave him a great welcome when he called on him Thursday evening. He brought him into his parlour and offered him his choice of drinks.

"I don't drink at all, thank you, never have."

"I'm so pleased to hear that. I know that drink had more than a little to do with our recent troubles, on both sides, actually...One prefers not to talk of such things. One tries to be charitable."

"The most charitable thing you can do in this case is tell the clean truth, as you see it."

"The truth is, Father, that he had the wool pulled over the people's eyes. He had the ordinary people literally eating out of his hand. They thought he could not do wrong. If Father Connor was to say that black was white, they would believe it from him. Don't ask me how he did it. It was as if he was pretending to be an ordinary man himself. You would never think he was a priest at all."

"You mean he did not fulfil his priestly duties?"

"Oh no, I am not saying that. Fair is fair. But he was too easygoing on the people. There was none of the cross or the fires of hell in his sermons. The complete opposite, actually: Do what you like. God will forgive everything. That might not be exactly the way he put it, but it came across like that to the people. All his talk was about a merciful God. You would think there was no devil at all. We will need a strong old-fashioned priest to bring back the faith in this place—no easy task."

"What do people think of Father Connor, at this point in time?"

"They know him now. They know him for what he is, a Judas."

"You would think he has no support among the people?"

"I'm not saying that. There are hardliners here and there, especially on the island, that would stand by him through thick and thin. They are people you wouldn't see at the altar too often, you understand, but they are very great with him."

"Are there many?"

"A good handful, the henchmen he had with him when they went up to picket the Dáil. You might have seen it on the television."

"What would people feel if he was to return again as your priest?"

"They would think—and forgive me for saying so—that our Lord Bishop was gone clean out of his mind."

"That's what I want to hear, the whole truth as it seems to you."

"The mistake the bishop made, if you pardon me saying so, was that he left him here saying mass and doing a burial, after he had been informed of the scandal. It gave the impression to the ordinary people that the Church authorities did not mind."

"Well...there were communication difficulties, and the dead have to be buried."

"Isn't it well that I managed to send word..."

"Yes, his Lordship is very appreciative, but he has to weigh up all aspects of the case before delivering his judgement. That is why he has sent me here to investigate fully."

Father Gilmore felt nervous before setting out to bring communion to the old and sick on Friday morning. Although a priest for twenty-four years, he had never worked in a parish and he was afraid he would not do things right. He need not have worried. He really enjoyed the day. He was welcomed to the houses, had old ladies kiss his hands. People were interested: Where was he from? Where was he working? Were his father and mother alive? Did he like this part of the country? Which did he prefer, the island or the mainland?

He found that views varied about Tom Connor— not everyone, not many really, were of like mind to Jack Jennings. He was often asked, "When will our own priest be back?" There were comments like, "This place is very lonely when you are on your own." "What is it except human nature?" "Isn't it better for them to keep the child and rear it than have it thrown into some home."

Not everyone would feel that he should be let back as priest but most said they would abide by the bishop's decision.

Anyone expecting a condemnatory sermon on the Sunday was disappointed. Peter Gilmore spoke on the day's gospel. He returned that evening to the city, his report ready for the bishop.

Tom Connor left Marion at her sister's house, and set out for the two main places of pilgrimage in his home county. He spent three days at Knock shrine praying that the Blessed Virgin Mary would intercede on his behalf with the Lord. He set out then for Croagh Patrick. The weather was beautiful but he had the mountain to himself. He had a tent and a primus stove, enough food for a few days. The beautiful view helped ease his mind: the great spread of Clew Bay, guarded by Clare Island, Achill to the north of it, Nephin to the north-east of him, the Twelve Pins and the mountains of Connemara to the south.

He was resigned now to leaving the priesthood. He would marry Marion immediately if she would accept. He knew that many laicised priests still said mass in their own homes. They could not live without it because they were priests forever, "like Melchizedek." He would be all right as long as he had the mass.

The bishop's hands were entwined like the roots of a tree.

"Sit down, Tom. How are you?"

"As well as can be expected, in the circumstances."

"Well..." He was nervous. He blurted out: "I have made my mind up to do as you asked me the last day. I will leave quietly. You will, please, arrange a laicisation as quickly as possible. I'm sorry..." He felt the tears well up.

"Tom. Do you remember the promise you made during your ordination when you placed your hands in the bishop's hands?"

"I do..."

"I am ordering you now to go back to your parish and continue the good work you have been doing."

"You're serious?"

"I will repeat myself if you wish."

"But...Marion. What about Marion?"

The bishop smiled. "I thought you were long enough in the priesthood, Tom, to be able to read between the lines."

"You're saying..."

"I'm not saying anything. You would hardly expect a bishop to incriminate himself...And Tom..." A little smile played about the episcopal lips. "No more babies."

"How exactly do I stand with regard to Marion and the child?" The bishop seemed to have lost interest. "What about Marion? Answer me, please." He pounded the table with his fist. "What about Marion...?"

He awoke, on the top of Croagh Patrick. It was raining. The rain merged with the cold sweat on his brow. He bundled his things together and hurried down the mountain.

When he called at Marion's sister's place, he found that she had left a few days previously. She had said nothing. She was gone one morning when they got up. He failed to find a trace of her anywhere.

The bishop's letter asked him to remove his personal effects as quickly as possible from the parish house. A replacement priest was ready to move in. He stood suspended from that day. The bishop regretted that he was not in a position to meet him. He had to take a holiday, at short notice, for the sake of his health.

Other Titles from Poolbeg

The Homesick Garden

by
Kate Cruise O'Brien

"That's the trouble with trying to get your parents to like each other. They get sentimental instead. Or edgy. By edgy I mean they start edging the conversation towards sex, they start telling you things you don't really want to know. Mum made me feel awkward. I knew there was a time before I was born but I wasn't sure I wanted to hear about it—that way. In any case I didn't really see why she should feel so grateful to Dad just because he let her have a baby. I was the baby after all. I think he was lucky. But there was no arguing with Mum in this mood. She was wallowing in the past, getting to like Dad fifteen years too late."

The voice of Antonia, watchful young narrator of *The Homesick Garden*, the brilliant first novel of Kate Cruise O'Brien.

POOLBEG

The No 1 Bestseller
City Girl

by
Patricia Scanlan

City Girl is the story of three women whose enduring
friendship survives all the changes in their lives.
Devlin is blonde, beautiful and privileged but her life
takes a completely unexpected course as a result of
an impulsive love-affair.
Caroline is sensitive and longs so much for love that
she rushes headlong into marriage.
Maggie is passionate, sensuous and fun-loving but
finds her wings clipped by the demands of
her husband and children.
City Girl is the gripping saga of three
modern city girls.

POOLBEG

The No 1 Bestseller
Apartment 3B

by
Patricia Scanlan

Luxurious, expensive Apartment 3B is for sale. Many
want it, only one can buy it. Its owner, Liz Lacey,
successful artist and darling of the jet set, is about to
make a dramatic change in her life.
Apartment 3B is the enthralling story of Liz Lacey and of
the men and women who come to view her apartment:
sophisticated, cosmopolitan Lainey Conroy; globe-
trotting media personality, Hugh Cassidy; gentle,
determined Claire Moran who has triumphed over
adversity; ambitious but tender-hearted Dominic Kent.
And Cecily, sister-in-law to Lainey, who will stop at
nothing to prevent Lainey from acquiring the apartment.

POOLBEG

Jimmy O'Dea

The Pride of The Coombe

by
Philip B Ryan

The definitive biography of Ireland's premier comic
actor, who died in 1965.

POOLBEG

Taisce Duan

A Treasury of Irish Poems with Translations in English

Edited by Sean McMahon and Jo O'Donoghue

A choice of poetry from both the literary and the folk
tradition, dating from the early 17th century to the early
20th century. The translators include some of modern
Ireland's foremost poets and scholars.

POOLBEG

Prisoners

The Civil War Letters of Ernie O'Malley

edited by
Richard English and Cormac O'Malley

Ernie O'Malley(1897-1957) was one of the most
charismatic figures to emerge from the 1916-1923
revolution in Ireland. He was converted to Republicanism
during the 1916 Rising and remained an influential
member of the IRA during both the Anglo-Irish War and
the Civil War. *On Another Man's Wound* and *The Singing
Flame*, his autobiographical accounts of the period, are
classics.

These previously uncollected letters, written while Ernie
O'Malley was imprisoned in 1923 and 1924, illuminate
this important period in modern Irish history.

POOLBEG